Miracle Nantze

A Novella

Daina Land

Kindle Direct Publishing

For my mother, Betty Jo Miller

Contents

Miracle Nantze

Daina Land

∞ ∞ ∞

Chapter One

The war in Crimea had robbed so many of so much that those who had the good fortune of staying in England found themselves unable to comprehend the horrors of those who had the misfortune not to die on the battlefield. Their disfigured bodies, their blank and vacant stares returned to the island in droves. Mothers, wives, and sweethearts who had counted themselves lucky, received their sons, husbands, and beaus back with adulation only to learn that a stranger had returned in their place. These strangers carried only a mere hint or occasional resemblance to the boys and men that had left them; therefore, not only were the soldiers confused and distraught, but so were their loved ones.

If you asked the men, it was, on the whole, the stench of death they could not remove from their nostrils. It was there when they finally nodded off of a night, and it was their first recognizable thought when they awoke. It traveled with them throughout their daily routine as they milked, milled, and managed their mundane lives. Nantze, however, was different due to one particular moment during the rush of battle that changed his perspective—changed his life.

A thick layer of fog had rolled inland off the Alba. The Turks were to hold the lines against the Russians and failed. Great losses, after two excruciating hours of the thunderous cannon beats, caused the Turks to turn tail and abandon the guns to the Russians. An event that caused their allies both disgust and great anguish.

Men's disfigured bodies had stymied the ground until it was slick with their blood, torn flesh, and dismembered limbs. Those able to dodge the carnage of an incoming cannon ball were required to prove their mettle in the clanking torment of hand to hand combat and this after cholera had razed the allies' troops by halves.

The dead or dying blue and bulging figures clad in their colorful French, British, and Highland uniforms lie as thick and intricately woven as Persian rugs. Under the deluge was Nantze, his right leg mangled and limp in its socket. The force of an iron ball had pitched him backwards and left him peering skyward as the battle raged around him like a violent, inescapable sea.

The sky, since the fog had lifted, ranged in shades of peaceful blue hues and large overstuffed clouds floated seaward. As Nantze watched, one cloud parted, a shaft of heavenly light lit upon his upturned face, and God spoke to him above the din of war. He'd heard Christ's thunderous whisper and knew without audibly hearing that God had plans for him, making Nantze's spirit rise in his chest and physically pull his body heavenward. Equally amazing was how swiftly his spirit settled within him, and the peace, spoken of as being like a river, comforted him. In an instant, he knew God had singled him out for life, and his fears left him. Pain, however, was not so kind, and within moments of the event, he succumbed to unconsciousness.

The reality of God's intervention on the battlefield, however, helped him as he lie near dead upon the blood soaked field, and as he waited for the medical convoy to take him to the Selimiye Barrack Hospital in Scutari near Istanbul. It helped him as he lie in the cholera infested hospital and as he endured the endless hours of excruciating pain when his wounds were cleansed and his infected leg removed.

Due to the lack of organization from the government, needed

supplies, clean beds, food, and medication were almost nonexistent. The doctors, nurses, and nuns marveled, however, at Nantze's stamina and disposition. Each time he was asked about his ability to smile at the difficulties that loomed before him, he replied with a wink and a sideways smile in his thick British accent, "God is my strength and stay. He didn't save me fer nothin'. I will, by God's grace, return to British soil."

They quite believed him. He radiated peace, often hobbling from his bed to his neighbor's to encourage, scribe, listen to a man's pleas, or whisper the firm and inextricably Word of God in his ear. The more he moved around the hospital the healthier he became. The doctors, each in turn and privately, asked him to stay as his release neared.

"Ya know, it does the men good ta see ya moving around," Brunsie, a doctor from Sussex, told him as he looked around the place at the number of men with amputees. "They're fresh out of hope here. Yours goes a long bloody way!"

"Bloody, now that's a poor choice o' words, isn't it Brunsie?" Nantze replied with a sideways glance at those very same men. "With a man like you wanderin' about the place, it's no wonder all these boys feel wrought with defeat. Ya go around disfigurin' hope as easily as the field surgeons disfigured bodies. Not only that, but ya have a bad habit of remindin' them of their limitations rather than their possibilities, is what I says."

"That is precisely why we, and more importantly THEY, need ya ta stay on," Brunsie added as he pointed with his thick thumb toward the bed-filled ward. "I cannot, fer the life of me, see beyond what they are ta what they can be."

"I say, that is very bad of ya! The only way ya could be less effective is if ya were ta become a man of the cloth!"

"Just so," the good doctor answered. "Now, what other talents do ya have? Surely ya were makin' a livin' prior ta joinin' the ranks? I need somethin' tangible that I can use ta justify keepin' ya on?"

Looking around at the many decrepit beds and supplies, the broken latches on the windows, and having already scratched out designs for a metal leg, Nantze explained, "I'm a damn good smithy! In fact, I've an idea how we might get these men on their feet."

He then explained to Brunsie, that prior to the war, he'd spent his life working the bellows and, as his mother phrased it, "tinkerin' with everythin' I could get my hands on!" Seeing that this gift was surprisingly needed in the barracks hospital, it was decided that he would stay on and work as a handyman of sorts, and as expected, he moved from patient to staff swiftly.

Having first-hand knowledge of what an amputee struggled with was valuable information. It helped Nantze design a leg unit that was durable, stiffly flexible, and inexpensive to make. The device included a porcelain bowl, a rubber mold made from a cast of the patient's stump, a metal joint and belt unit, and a metal leg and foot unit. It was not boasted to be a thing of beauty; however, it was a quick and easy way to get a man back up on his feet and home. It wasn't until a man stood upright that his hope returned, and in their position, hope was the only thing that was going to help them.

Because of his skill and disposition, many of the men whom he came in contact with began to thrive. It did their hearts good to see his contraption. Every man he showed it to had the same response, "Ya think ya can make me one of those things?"

Nantze would shrug his shoulders and say, "I'll give it a go, but you'll have to get upright. I can't blood well measure ya fer it while yer lyin' down, now can I?"

This was all the encouragement the men needed. They began to struggle against the bed and wage war with the chair. They'd pull, hop, and strain against restraints in an effort to wobble around the place like Nantze had done.

This work kept him busy until the close of the hospital; however, once back on British soil, there seemed no place for a one-leg smithy with the gift of encouragement, so he was a bit of a transient until he finally settled in Lancaster, working for a man named Wilmarth. Over the course of some time and because he was able to get his hands upon better supplies, Nantze made a number of improvements to his original prosthetic until it was almost comfortable.

∞∞∞

On the River Eden in Carlisle, England just south of Scotland, lie a blacksmith's shop. A man named Cinead Christison, or Cin as he was called, worked the bellows of the same smithy shop as his father and his father before him. He was a large man of Nordic and Scottish descent, a highlander as was his son, who was equally named but instead went by the name of Cinny. Their family had been smithies for as long as anyone could remember, and being Nordic-Scots and big-bodied, able men capable of wielding a hammer for hours on end, they were built for the work.

These two men were ruled by one small nymph of a girl, Christison's daughter, Katie, who was as petite as they were brawny. Both, however, cowered to the powerful tongue lashings she was capable of wielding when crossed. They ate heartily, worked heartily, and walked softly where the girl was concerned.

She was the only other member left of the family. Her mother, Catherine, had died years before as had all the other children born to Christison. Katie's love for the men, however, propelled her sharp tongue on more than one occasion, and without fail, they attended the Carlisle Cathedral on Sundays and carted her to market on Mondays. Theirs was a succinct family unit. One wheel did not turn without the motion of the others nor was there a greater love, and without a doubt, Katie's was the love that kept everything in motion.

The girl could boast of a massive amount of chestnut colored locks, lashes, and brows. All of which outlined her large doe-shaped, blue-green eyes. Her mother, being of Scandinavian heritage, had taught the girl to braid her hair so that it wrapped becoming around her head and weighed less heavily upon her neck, which produced so many headaches for girls similarly blessed with such abundant locks. Her hair, however, combined with her petite size, dwarfed her considerably, making her look elfin and sprite-like.

∞∞∞

Not far from the smithies lived a man by the name of Palfrey, not Mr. Palfrey, not Joe or James or John Palfrey—just Palfrey. In fact, no one had ever heard him called by his given name nor had anyone ever even heard of him offering one. His once dark, Irish hair was now white and wild. His most striking feature, however, were his eyebrows, for over his piercing, bright blue eyes sat twin brows like black-tipped, furry caterpillars. Each of which rose and fell with every animated word he spoke.

This same Palfrey was awakened at dawn by the reverberating hoof beats of a rider, whipping up dirt and fear, which settled upon the old man's superstitious mind until a horrid feeling of dread filled him, making him hasten his spry, crooked little body to the window in time to see a black-cloaked rider and steed plummet at a breakneck speed through the small thoroughfare that ran past his cottage off the small hamlet road. The rider's morbid-looking cape flew angrily behind him, which in Palfrey's mind foretold of coming doom.

Seeing the figure, the old man crossed himself and said a prayer, thankful the shrouded ghoul had not turned and directed his toxic gaze at him as he thundered by. Had such an event happened, Palfrey knew, as any other man would have, that his time on earth had come to an end; however, since he had raced on without one look in the old man's direction, Palfrey believed himself to be safe. Knowing this and recovering from the shock, however, were two entirely different matters. Visibly shaking, the old man hurried back to bed and shook his wife, Ivy.

"Wake up woman! I saw an omen!" he whispered harshly. Filled with a palpable fear, the twin caterpillars above his eyes began to tremble.

"Ahh, Palfrey, ya ol' duffer! Damn ya if ya hadn't woken me up now! Couldn't let me sleep in peace, could ya? Had ta go flappin' that ever-movin' jaw o' yers and sprinkle yer fear around the room like powder!" she began as his penetrating fear encompassed her reprise. "It's yer mother's Irish blood that makes ya jump at every stray leaf, thinkin' it's an omen, it is!" She prattled on, working up a good steam, but when the man that cuddled up next to her quaked in her arms, she stifled her barrage of words and became instantly concerned.

To hear her tell it, the two had been married an incalculable amount of time and had weathered, withered, and been woven together over the course of so many years that there was no fixed date that either of them could recall or agree upon for their actual anniversary. It mattered little how much time had passed. She only knew that in all the years she had known him, Palfrey had never quaked like an infant; therefore, she held him and gave the old man permission to rattle away as he liked without any chastisement from her.

Later, after the sun had risen in its sphere, Katie, having long been expecting her family's return, decided to walk to where the hamlet road intersected the main road to Carlisle. As she reached the bend in the road, she happened upon a collision. Looking around at the carnage, she was able to make out two lifeless forms.

Their battered bodies lie crumpled at nightmarishly hideous angles. One man's bones protruded from his skin. The marrow and sinew, having popped and splattered, littered the ground around with splintered bone. The other man's cap was split by the nearby rock wall that ran the whole length of the lane. Having come upon such a gruesome scene, it took some moments before she was able to deduce their identities.

It was the horse that brought her to her discovery. The frothing beast lie on his side whinnying, blood filling his nostrils. At intervals, he snorted, splattering crimson froth upon the road. It was the same horse she had ridden as a girl. The same horse that pulled their cart. In fact, it was also the same horse that had taken her father and brother to the train station early that morning before the sun came up to collect a massive contraption that needed some style of work done to it, which the railroad had hired the men to do.

The shock of this realization caused Katie to look around frantically for other clues. Lying some ways away from the flatbed cart was a large black mass of metal, which Katie could only assume was the item they'd gone to the station to retrieve. It had broken loose its cords and, no doubt, aided in the accident. Her father's leather apron, too, lay haphazardly on the ground as did a scattering of his tools and the leather bag he'd taken with him. Seeing that there was now no doubt of the men's identity, she began to retch uncontrollably.

When Palfrey had come upon the horrid scene some little time later and discovered Katie lying some ways away, he thought she had been miraculously thrown from the cart and thus saved. The vomit that covered her dress, however, was a mystery that was not solved until sometime later when it was learned that she had not been present when the accident happened.

News traveled quickly, as it always does, and Death—as he always does— drew a crowd. Each of which performed some small duty to clear the site. Pine boxes were made, items were gathered from the ground and surrounding area where they'd been flung, and the horse and cart were burned on site to avoid disease and the difficulty of burying such a large animal. The contraption Cin and son had gone to the train station to retrieve was also carted off the road and put outside the smithy shop.

The Christison men had been, after all, known in the area as hard-working men of principle, quiet giants who were as willing to build a contraption to spec as they were to rework a plow or sharpen a scathe, so it was little wonder that the town's people each aided Kate in their own small way.

After their burial, Katie lie on her side spent, breathing in gasps and unable to compensate for the uncontrollable pain.

Since the time of her father and brother's deaths, it had been etched deeply along the lines of her lips. It encircled her hard, red eyes. Gone now, all of them and with no other family member to work the forge, it was obvious that she would be forced to sell or hire a man to work her father's forge. As far as Kate was concerned, she much preferred to join them in the family's plot located near a sleepy, little glen at the Carlisle cemetery.

It took less time, however, for the town to recover. The Christisons had not, as of yet, been in the ground a fortnight when the men folk started talking about the need for a new smithy. Cin was a good man, but people still needed their carts mended and iron-work done; therefore, after the Christison's affairs were settled, the men of the small hamlet area outside of Carlisle proper met at the Yellow Sow, as they did most nights, to discuss the going-ons of those who lived in the area.

On this particular night, the only talk bouncing around the pub was the accident and what was to be done about the fiery little lass, Katie Christison. They all agreed that she would need the income, so like it or not, she was going to have to hire a man. They gave the job of telling the girl this news to Palfrey because they knew she'd succumb to his prodding and because they were all a little afraid of her.

Besides that, Palfrey, for all his being an animated character and a lover of a high handed tale or two, had her best interest at heart. They all did, and after much deliberation, discussion, and debate, their decisions were that the girl needed an income, they needed a smithy, and Palfrey needed another pint. So they riled up the curate, a one Thomas Merriweather, to get him to pen a request to The London Times and The Edinburgh Evening Courant.

"Now boys, what kind of smithy do we want ta be givin' this prime livin' ta?" Palfrey began as the owner of the Yellow Sow, Kincaid, sought out a scrap of paper and pen for Merriweather.

Receiving both, the somewhat stodgy and portly curate answered, "First and foremost," he began but then paused thoughtfully, "he must be a man of good moral character. We don't want a man who will come and attempt to defraud us."

"Or take advantage of our Katie," Palfrey added.

"One cross word outta Kate, and he'll soon learn ta keep his place," Kincaid reminded the men, and they all laughed.

"In that case, better make him a stout-hearted fellow. One who's battle-worn." Shot out Jimmy MacMarker, who'd once tried to hold Katie's hand when he was eleven and walked home with a black eye.

With a knowing wink at Kincaid, Palfrey called out over the top of his raised jar, "Tell us again Jimmy, what was it ya told yer mum when ya had come home with that shiner? A gang of thieves was it?" The sound of laughter filtered through the air, relieving the men's tension like a wave.

"Battle-worn ya say? Must be some men what's made it out of Crimea, surely."

"Not enough, God rest 'em," Kincaid answered.

A small pause was observed, then all the men raised their jars simultaneously and chanted, "Aye!" in a toast to the dead and returned soldiers. Their glasses, likewise, landed in unison, and another short pause was observed out of respect before they continued their business.

"We need a man what can do the work of two. Cin and son were a well-oiled machine, puttin' out products like MacMurphy's wife there pops out wee ones." MacMurphy smiled, raising his sideburns a full inch off his cheeks and making his facial hair look like it stood at attention.

"He'll need ta provide references," Pippen the Tailor quipped, "Don't forget about that."

"Aye, aye and provide a list of accomplishments," Pippen the Sweep, his twin brother, piped in.

"We don't want no fly-by-night jobs being done here. What we need is someone who's accomplished at his craft," the curate added as he scribbled down a quick list of requirements for the new smithy.

The advertisement was then handed to Mr. Hardy, the postmaster, who read it out loud. "Needed one accomplished blacksmith, who can do the job of two. Send accomplishments and references in care of Thomas Merriweather, Carlisle, Cumbria," he called out in a clear voice. "I'll get the squire to frank them in the mornin' when he comes," he told the crowd after he further inspected the document.

The quiet of the pub was undisturbed for a brief moment until a man, the locals called the Londoner, spoke up. "I knows a man what's back from the war," the Londoner began. "Name's Nantze. Got one leg. had it blown off, e' did. Made a fearful lookin' metal leg fer himself. Ingenious is what I calls it. In-gen-ious," he thundered away, dropping subjects, predicates, and consonants as he went. "He's the man ya need here," he told them, paused, then spoke again. "Stayed in Turkey fer a time makin' metal legs fer men what lost their kickers. Started callin' him a miracle worker. Yup, Miracle Nantze they calls him."

Here the Londoner paused again for a drink. "Yes, siree. They say he did more ta rally morale by makin' legs than the priests could do with all their prayers," he rattled off, cradling his ale under his lips until he met with a pause. He was just about to take another swig when he noticed the curate seated nearby and so lowered his glass a moment. "No offense ta the cloth," he added, then proceeded to finish his jar and ask for a refill with a tap of his finger on his glass.

"Where's this Nantze bloke now?" asked Palfrey, mimicking the Londoner's tap for a refill. While Kincaid answered their requests, the Londoner continued.

"Livin' in Lancaster. Railcar sprung some spring or somethin' on the way here one day, and they calls him in ta do the quickie and get us back on the road."

"Well, he's as welcome ta apply as any. Besides that, we could all do with a miracle," announced the curate with a nod.

"Might very well need a miracle man ta keep Kate from weepin' herself ta an early grave, and if he's as good as ya says he is, we'd be obliged if ya'd send him word when ya go back through Lancaster," added Kincaid as he handed him his ale.

"Aye, I'll pass the word along."

"Now that's what I calls a good night's work," Pippen the

Sweep chimed, drawing the pub owner's attention to his glass.

"Pippen the Sweep," Kincaid called out. "Ya aimin' ta drink that ale or rock it ta sleep?" he asked with a knowing wink at Palfrey. The man made no response but lifted the jar to his lips and drew a long draught, causing the men around him to roar with laughter.

"Now how in the world is it that yer constantly called Pippen the Sweep?" asked the Londoner. "I been comin' ta this here pub fer a bit now, and ya is always bein' called Pippen the Sweep. Seems an odd fancy ya near-Scots have about bestowin' names upon each other."

"We call him that ta ward off any confusion," Jeffers, a man that reminded most people of a bulldog, explained and then waited for the Londoner to respond, which he did.

"What confusion?"

"Well, now we're not London folk here, so forgive us our trifles, but it was the only way ta keep from being mixed up with his brother."

"Who he be?" asked the Londoner, obviously confused.

"Pippen the Tailor," Jeffers explained with a broad smile.

Pippen the Tailor, sitting next to his likeness at the bar, popped his head out from behind his brother. "Sees what he means," he called out to the Londoner.

"I can't say that helped do anythin' more than muddy unclear water," the Londoner slurred, not making the connection before raising his glass again.

"Well with as many pints as you've downed, I can quite easily believe you," reprimanded the curate as he gathered his effects and headed for the door—his business being completed. Pulling his eyes away from his glass long enough to watch the hoity-toity man exit, the Londoner looked back down the bar at Pippen the Sweep. This time, however, both brothers turned to look at him in unison, and his eyes bulged dramatically.

"I'm seein' twice as much as I should be!" he tottered, motioning in a series of semicircles on his seat, making the twins chuckle.

With the curate's exit, the conversations returned to their usual less philanthropic topics, and soon the small room was filled with the sound of men's laughter, rumbling and bouncing around between the wooden beams and the flagstone floor.

Before long the fire dwindled down, and the pub became cool. "Well now boys it's about time." Kincaid, wiping down the long wooden bar, said and began to nod men towards the door.

"Time fer what?" murmured the Londoner.

"Lockin' up," returned Kincaid.

"How can ya tell?" he slurred, wobbling his head noticeably.

Pointing at the man seated next to him at the bar, he told him, "When those caterpillars o' Palfrey's start crawlin' across his face on their own, it's time ta call it a night."

Looking over at Palfrey, who was wiggling his eyebrows up and down, the Londoner attempted to focus. "They be dancin' a jig, alright."

The men, having seen Palfrey's display, chuckled again and pulled themselves off their seats, scraping the chair legs along the flagstone floor as they stood and emptied the content of their jars before shuffling toward the door.

∞∞∞

Chapter Two

Over the course of the next few weeks, the men received and discussed numerous responses to their advertisement. None, however, seemed enough to lure them into accepting one over the other, so their search continued. Katie, too, was anxious. Fearful of the men choosing a man too quickly over a jar of ale, she rode them not to be too hasty. Fearful of Katie, the men took their time and checked on a few of the candidate's references via a letter to the local clergy to ask about the man's moral character.

The Londoner, having remembered his promise to tell Nantze about the position when he went back through Lancaster, sought the man out. It took little time to find him, he only needed to follow the pings of the hammer.

The local smithy in Lancaster, a one Thomas Wilmarth, was a large, well-fed man, who liked to watch Nantze work more than help him, and since he was the owner of the establishment, it was his prerogative to do so. He offered Nantze a good living for a single man. He had his wage, of course, a comfortable room above the blacksmith's shop, and meat enough to fuel a man of his stature on his plate three times a day. For Nantze it was a good arrangement, but that didn't mean that he wouldn't accept something better if it came along; therefore, when he was approached by a stout, somewhat-respectable-looking fellow, he took the idea seriously.

"Oy, Nantze, there!" The Londoner offered with an upraised arm, coming into the sweltering smithy shop. Seeing him, Nantze stopped his hammer mid-stroke and gave the man his full attention. "I be a regular in these parts. Saw yer work a time or two. Name's Tiddle. Come ta tell ya of a livin' up in Carlisle."

"Well, now I'm right glad." Putting down his tool, he wiped his hands on his streaked leather apron and raked a handkerchief across his forehead and around his neck. "What happen ta the smithy they had?"

The heat in the smithy shop settled like bricks in the Londoner's lungs, making him wheeze uncomfortably, but he grabbed a mouthful air just the same and let loose his announcement. "Had two. Father and son. Cin and Cinny they called 'em. Dead. Both of them. Carriage crashed. Splintered bones and blood ev'rywhere. Damn horrible sight. Lookin' fer a replacement. Said I'd pass the news on. So I did. Man of my word, I am!" Tiddle finished up, following Nantze's example by wiping the sweat from across his brow.

"Well, now that is bad news indeed."

"Fer those two blokes! Might work ta yer advantage, though, eh?" Tiddle added and offered Nantze a coarse looking smile.

"Where's the forge?"

"It were a family shop. Down the hamlet road."

"Might I find a bed there?"

"Aye, I'd think so. They wants a smithy, sure enough. Be fools ta invite ya and not offer ya a bed, is what I says!" Then plopping the London Times with the advertisement circled numerous times with a pencil down on a nearby workstation and sopping his brow, the Londoner added, "Address if ya wanna reply."

"Thank ya much, Tiddle." Stretching out his soiled hand, Nantze shook the man's chubby fist before that fellow tootled himself off the way he came. For the rest of the day, Nantze thought about a possible move. The more he imagined having the run of a shop without a boss the more he liked the idea.

In fact, when at closing time, Wilmarth came in and told him to finish up a job that could wait until tomorrow, Nantze was quite positive he'd like the idea of being his own man all the more. It might not be difficult for a normal man to stay on his feet for hours on end, but for a bloke with only one good leg, it was a real trial. Working that hard put his stump on the alert, then it was all fire and heat to pay until he could soothe and rest it.

Therefore, after hearing about the need in Carlisle and feeling keenly an unction to go, he wrote a letter inquiring into the position. Receiving a reply, Nantze, urged by some inner workings of the Almighty, sent word that he'd make the short trip by rail to meet the men and stay a few days if they'd like to see his craftsmanship first hand, causing the group of them to look forward to meeting the man and seeing the wondrous contraption he'd made for himself; therefore, making his excuses to Wilmarth and explaining that he had personal business to take care of, he made arrangements to go.

On the day of his trip, Nantze saw a familiar face at the train station. Jim Hutchins had hired him to do a few odd jobs for the railroad on occasion. With a raised arm and a brief wave, Hutchins called out, "Nantze! Well now, if ya aren't the very man I was talkin' ta Mr. Cummings about." Hutchins offered with a flip of his thumb in the railroad man's direction as the two walked over to the ticket counter to talk to Nantze. Once the two came up and stood beside him, Hutchins continued, "Cummings here is needin' a smithy and wants ta offer ya a full-time position workin' fer the line."

"Does he?" Nantze replied, looking over the dandified gent. His manner of dress was all poppy-cocks and horse flesh, making Nantze doubt the man cared for much more than the thickness of his purse and the contents of his plate. Most likely, he'd want to run Nantze cross country doing odd jobs on one iron contraption after another without much thought to what it might cost a one-leg man.

"I told him how ya was!" Cummings continued with a broad smile, feeling very much like Providence was on his side.

"How am I?" Nantze asked, looking Hutchins in the eye.

"You're a man what can be counted on ta do his work, that's what! Moreover, that's just the kinda bloke what's needed fer this here prime livin'."

"A prime livin', is it?" Nantze asked with upturned brows. "And just how much does this here 'prime livin' pay?"

Hutchins, grinning at Cummings, popped off, "Now there, sir, dinna I tell ya the man was all business. 'He wants ta know how much!"

"Fifty pounds per annum," Cummings announced, looking proudly at Nantze as if he'd offered him a veritable fortune.

With very little thought, Nantze parried, "Best ta make it twice as much. I can make more than that runnin' my own forge!" Nantze, having paid for his ticket and got his change from the attendant, nodded at the fellow. "Obliged," he told the fellow with a quick, easy smile.

"Well now! That is a sum! Don't know that it could be managed!" Cummings hemmed until Nantze turned and looked him in the eye. "I suppose it depends upon whether ya want yer train ta run or sit idle," answered Nantze, coming to the point of the conversation with a smile before leaving the two men to follow him as he walked toward the boarding dock. "I'm now on my way ta Carlisle ta see 'bout takin' over as the local smithy."

"What's that? Yer plannin' on goin' north?" Removing the hat from his head, Hutchins swiped a handkerchief across his brow.

"Aye, I'll go where I'm best paid!" As he spoke, he continued his lumbering gait to the waiting iron giant. "I'm a man what needs ta work, that's fer sure, but just as surely, I'm a man what will take advantage of the best situation! Beyon' that, I can easily imagine the railroad not carin' over much how many hours it keeps me on my bum leg, eh?"

"How long will ya be gone?" Hutchins asked, taken aback. Evidently he thought Nantze would be delighted with the opportunity.

"Unsure. I imagine they'd like ta see what I can do. Maybe some few days or a week till I return."

"Well now, I'll not hold the job forever!" Cummings crowed.

"Nor have I asked ya ta. Right good day ta ya both!" Nantze told the men in parting as he tipped his felt hat to the pair.

As he lumbered away toward the waiting train, the conductor called out, "All aboard!" The fellow bellowed this phrase numerous times in succession, causing those in the station's sitting area to herd toward an open door.

The loading dock, constructed of a covered, paved walkway, filled with a cloud of steam as the engineer pulled upon the pressure release valve. The noise made from the large, steam engine rattled back and forth between the station and the train cars, exciting Nantze a little.

He could easily admit that the idea of working on such a fantastic beast was appealing. There were more gears, switches, valves, and forged metal on it than could be found virtually anywhere else, making it as thrilling an escapade for a grown man as could be imagined.

Nantze considered the conversation as he hobbled to get in line and board the train. He hoped that he'd played his cards well with Cummings. The railroad was a damn rough taskmaster, and everyone knew it. He also knew they were more in need of a smithy than he was in need of a job.

In fact, the railroad was notorious for offering a low bid and hoping the poor bloke was desperate enough to take it. He'd seen them do it to a handful of men. Still, they had a right to offer what they wanted. They were the bloody railroad.

Nantze, however, knew his craft, and the idea of being his own master was very appealing for a man who was used to taking orders. Wouldn't hurt Cummings to wait on ice for a day or two either. It might even work out for his benefit if the pampered railroad man thought he was willing to walk, or in his case, hobble away in search of a better opportunity.

Having had to travel through a few cars to find his seat, his metal leg clanked and groaned as he clamored slowly along. Those behind and about him desired to ask why he rattled, but as was always the case, they only gaped wide-eyed and rudely. Ready to rest, Nantze finally settled himself in an empty row of chairs for the northern trek.

A boy, occupying the seat across the small walkway from him and being of an inquisitive age, began noticing the strange way in which Nantze's trousers fell upon his missing leg. At first the boy examined him, next he considered a series of questions, and then finally, to his mother's horror, the question that was on all of the passengers' minds popped out of his mouth rather too loudly to be polite.

"Where's yer leg?"

"Well, now, I don't rightly know," Nantze replied as he waited for the boy's next question, which he was sure would be forthcoming.

"How can ya not know where yer leg is?" he asked with his face skewed sideways in confusion.

"Well, I guess I never asked."

With a nod that said that was a good enough answer for the boy, he pointed at Nantze's pants. "What ya got under there then?"

"A metal leg." Nantze looked at the boy's mother. Censure, primed and aimed at her son's questions clear and present upon her rose colored cheeks allowed Nantze to smile reassuringly at her. "He's just a lad. Besides that, it's healthy fer a boy ta want ta experiment with the world."

Receiving nothing more than, "Hmmph!" from that good lady, Nantze did his best to encourage the boy.

Seeing that Nantze was understanding of his inquisitive nature, the boy blurted out, "Can I see it?"

Pulling up his pant leg, Nantze smiled. "Sure, I made it myself, so don't judge too harshly, eh?"

"I won't," the boy promised with a quirky sort of nod and an excited grin. He'd never seen such a thing and couldn't imagine how it might work, and wouldn't Jimmy Timmons be surprised to find out that he'd met a man with a metal leg.

Unhooking the contraption, Nantze laid it across his lap and showed the boy how the knee bent and ankle joint bounced slightly. "That's ta help offer a little cushion ta the stump."

"Does it hurt?"

"Yes."

"Was it blown off in the war?" he asked a little too excitedly.

"Yes."

"What's the end of yer leg look like?"

Rolling up his pants to the stump, he let the boy take a look. It was a damn gruesome sight. The flesh was bruised. The scars, too, were bright pink and raised up off of the rest of the skin.

"Looks like the very devil, doesn't it?" the boy offered, mimicking a phrase he learned from his father and ignoring a cross look from his mother, which was another thing he learned from his father.

"Yes, it does." Rubbing the boy's head, Nantze smiled before re-attaching the leg unit.

Having had all his questions answered and being thoroughly intrigued by his new knowledge, the boy took out his sketch book and drew a crude representation of what he'd learned followed by an entire flip book of cartoon pictures of Nantze getting his leg blown off in the war.

Not caring to relive the event via moving still life, Nantze pulled down his cap, crossed his arms over his large chest, and attempted to get some much needed rest. As soon as he closed his eyes, however, he could hear the boy's mother spitting fire at him for embarrassing her. The lad, unaffected by his mother's rants so often as he'd heard them, continued to scribble away in his journal and say such things as, "Look at this mum," and "Won't Jimmy be surprised I met a man with a metal leg!"

Coming to a halt in Carlisle, hiring a rig for the ride, and making his way to the Yellow Sow as his letter required, Nantze arrived at the pub, hoping to get a belly full of whatever he could and rest his leg a bit before the men came to scrutinize his abilities at the bellows.

Hopping down from the rig, tying up the horse, and pulling down his duffel, Nantze hobbled into the pub, looked around a bit, and carried himself over to one of a pair of brocade stuffed chairs by the fire. In between the twin chairs, a small wooden table resided and before it, stood a large, round wooden table covered in scuff marks.

Seeing him when he entered, Kincaid called out, "Well now, Nantze is it?"

The suction that held the leg to his stump hadn't been right since he'd reattached it on the train. There just wasn't enough room to finagle the unit as he normally was able to, making him limp lopsided and rub on an area of skin that wasn't calloused. "Aye, mind if I reset my leg a minute?" he asked in obvious discomfort.

"Not a bit, not a bit. Was hopin' ta get an ogle of that leg of yours. I hears it's a mechanical marvel!" Kincaid told him, making Nantze think he was almost as excited to see his device as the boy on the train.

"Hopefully, he won't draw out a picture representation of it flyin' through the air ta show his friends!" he joked with himself before saying, "Well, that is high praise, indeed. Undeserved, but I'll take it." Then settling himself in the chair and rolling up his trouser leg, he asked, "Ya have a glass of ale for me, I suppose, and mayhap a meal?"

"Already dishin' it up," Kincaid offered, moving behind the bar to get it ready. Pulling the lid off of a pot of stew, ladling it into a large bowl, and adding it to a tray that already contained a thick slice of buttered bread, cheese, and Kincaid's famous ale, he came around the bar to where Nantze sat and plopped the heavily laden tray on the table.

"Well, now that's what I calls quick." Taking in the proffered meal, Nantze took a swig or two of his ale and finished unhooking his leg. Handing the contraption to Kincaid, who turned it over in his hands as he inspected it, Nantze bowed his head respectfully, offered up his silent thanks to the Lord Jesus Christ, and partook of the best meal he'd had in some time. In between mouthfuls, he answered Kincaid's questions

"How'd ya think ta use a porcelain bowl?" Kincaid asked.

"That was no magic. It was just what they brought my gruel in while I was in the barrack hospital."

"And this rubber seal, how'd ya manage that?"

"Had ta make a cast, of course, so I put plaster in the bowl and made an impression of the stump. That rubber seal provides the suction needed ta keep it on."

"Heard ya made an army of these legs," Kincaid offered in obvious awe.

"Yes, well sadly they were required," Nantze replied, a little shaken by the reality of his words. "Those were difficult days, seein' all manner of men disfigured and hopeless. I shouldn't ever like ta see it again."

Feeling he should move on to another topic, Kincaid asked, "Well now, how'd ya learned such craft?"

"I've just always liked ta tinker with things, I suppose. Used ta drive me mum wild. She'd come home, and I'd have taken apart all the clocks, gas lamps, or door handles. So ta keep me out of mischief, she lent me ta the smithy down the street. When the old man started sendin' me home with a coin or two in my pocket, my mother was right glad she'd done so. I was eager fer learnin' in those days."

Nantze, stopping at intervals to either take a swig of ale or shovel in a mouthful of stew, spoke in the clear even terms of a hardworking man, causing Kincaid to like him almost instantly. "Once I was older, I was sacked off ta be educated like every other English schoolboy. There was a man there what fixed things. Threw me out of his shop more than once afore he decided ta put me ta work stokin' the fires, bendin' metal, and aidin' him about the place."

The memory of his childhood being thus exhumed, Nantze smiled, transforming his face dramatically. "The man, Dimwitty, he was, was a wiry ol' toad and not one ta talk over much. Never told me how ta do a thing. Instead, e'd show me a time or two, we'd do the task together, and lastly, he'd watch as I aped what'd he done. If'n I did it wrong, the ol' man would click his tongue, and I'd try a different tactic."

Watching him as he ate his meal and told his tale, Kincaid took stock of Nantze. As far as his appearance went, he was a downright handsome bloke. Knowing Katie as well as he did, Kincaid wasn't certain if that would aid or hinder him. She might take it into her head to distrust him.

Pulling his watch from his breeches' pocket, Kincaid offered, "Well now, won't be long, and the men'll come 'round fer a pint. They're all quite keen on meetin' ya."

"Who's this owner I must impress?" Nantze asked around another mouthful, referring to a portion of the letter he'd received, which said that the job being offered was subject to the scrutiny of the owner.

"Well now, that's a point of significance that I might as well tell ya about, I suppose." Kincaid leaned back upon the high-backed cushion of his chair, put his feet up, and took out his pipe before continuing. Not being prepared to tell Nantze about Kate, he wanted to think about the best way to explain her. Taking his time filling his pipe, the bar owner tossed out a few words about the girl.

"She's a mighty cunnin' lil' thin' what's just been bereft of her father and brother. Both were the smithies, Cin and son or the Cinnies as a lot of folks 'round here called 'em. She's a fire on a good day. Now with so much sorrow on her plate, she..." Kincaid paused a moment, drawing on his pipe and thinking of the right words to explain the issue when Palfrey shuffled in.

Thankful for the intrusion, Kincaid turned to Nantze. "This ol' bloke here is Palfrey," he offered as an introduction, but then asked the spry, furry headed fellow his opinion. "We be talkin' of Kate. Now how would ya describe our lil' issue with the lass?"

"She has us scared near ta death," Palfrey offered. His merry blue eyes dimmed by such sadness made his bushy eyebrows droop.

"Scared she'll close the smithy shop?" Nantze asked in confusion.

"Worse, scared she'll join Cin and son in the family plot." Palfrey swiped his handkerchief across his damp eyes in one swift motion and shook his head.

"Truth is, we all needs the smithy, but what's more, she needs the smithy," Kincaid explained before he added, "Won't have a groat ta her name 'less she hires a man, which she's too broken up ta do."

"So us men's decided ta do it fer her," Palfrey continued.

"But I have ta pass inspection?" Nantze asked, catching on to the meat of their meaning.

"Right!" both Kincaid and Palfrey nodded pleased he didn't require a greater explanation.

"I can do that!"

"She's a wild cat!" Kincaid offered quickly. "You must walk on tender feet."

"Well, in yer case, Nantze," the old fellow smiled, raising his twin eyebrows in a mischievous arch. "I says tender foot!" Palfrey, proud of his joke, swatted Kincaid's large shoulder and laughed.

The old fellow's personality was infectious, and Nantze instantly liked him. It was obvious he cared for the girl, and if those bushy eyebrows were any sign of the man's innate sense of humor, he was sure he'd get on well with him. Not only that, he thought it honorable that the men were willing to care for the girl.

"Pray, how old is she?"

"Three and twenty."

"Is she repellent then?" Nantze asked, wondering why she wasn't married.

"Listen ta him!" Palfrey spouted, waving his arm and slapping his hand against Kincaid's shoulder again. "Is she repellent, indeed! Repellent would be a welcomed compliment fer this here lass!" he offered with a wink at Kincaid. "Girl'll be round soon. Told her ya were comin' and ta stop in. You'll see fer yerself what kinda lass she be." Smiling and showing off his lack of dental hygiene over the years, Palfrey's eyes sparkled brightly, and his bushy brows seemed to giggle a little.

"Right, no matter what though," Kincaid added, "make sures ya don't send the girl in a tizzy by starin' at her lazy eye!"

"That's right, besides a handsome bloke like ya might sweeps a lass like that off her feet, and afore ya know it, ya gots yer own little smithy!" Palfrey threw out to see what kind of response the man would make. He seemed an upright fellow, but one could never really tell a thing about a man until he understood his motives.

"What kind of man do ya take me fer? I've no mind ta marry, so I can steal from an orphaned spinster. I've more spine than that!"

Nodding then at Kincaid, Palfrey smiled, sending the two caterpillar brows up. "That's a right smart answer, says me."

"It's a right truthful answer. I'm a man who believes in God, and I won't be havin' ya think I've clamped onto a motive I ain't got!"

"You'll need ta be!" Kincaid told him. "A man of God, that is. The girl's got a tongue like a whip." With both men smiling, Kincaid rose from his chair, gathered up the empty tray, and returned to the bar. Any moment now the men would be trickling in, and he needed to prepare for his regulars.

∞∞∞

Chapter Three

Before too much longer one man after another, toting his own jar or cup or mug, shuffled into the pub. Each was introduced to Nantze, who smiled, nodded, and sipped on his ale. It wasn't long before they asked to see his handiwork, and his leg was removed again and passed around the room for inspection.

"Well now, that seems ta me ta be a feat of engineerin' marvel," MacMurphy offered, looking at the mechanism that caused some give to the ankle.

Palfrey, seeing where he might use his joke again, replied, "Tis not, it be a foot of it!"

"Well, it's a leg up in any case!" Pippen the Tailor popped off as he took a gulp from his jar. Thinking it unfair that his twin let out the words that were still rattling around in his brain-cage, Pippen the Sweep nudged his brother in the ribs. "You knowed I was gonna say that!"

"Mayhap, but ya dinna get it out quick enough now did ya?" was his brother's rejoinder before he, too, ribbed his twin.

"Well then Nantze, what other kinds of contraptions can you make?" the curate asked, looking at the leg and wanting to make sure the men did their duty by hiring a competent and moral man to replace Cin and son.

"Well, sir, it depends upon the job that's needin' ta be done, but I've mended the mechanical mechanisms on the steam powered tractor, curricles, buggies, and all manner of rigs. The railroad has asked me ta fix and reattach the workings of the engine, pins, gears, and hand railings, and I've made more fences, handles, and knobs than I can count."

"Can ya make and mend a plow?"

"Aye," Nantze smiled, thinking that if he could mend a steam engine, he'd better be an expert at plows.

"What about making an iron gate? The Cinnies were restoring the cathedral's eight foot wrought iron fence before..." However, the words died on the curate's lips when the pub door opened, and all turned to see a tiny figure outlined by light from the setting sun.

In fact, the talking stopped all together, and each man froze in his place as the small frame of Katie Christison came into view, looked around, and settled her large doleful eyes on Nantze, who was at that moment balancing on his one good leg while one or another of the men were examining his fake leg, shoe and all.

Seeing her as she came into the light, Nantze's breath froze in his throat. Dressed all in black with a look of sorrow etched across her brow that could melt even a cruel man's reserve, she looked lost. Her dress, too, hung on her tiny frame like a weight.

The men, most of whom had not seen her since the Cinnies had been laid to rest, noticed her diminishing size, too, and stood gaping at her as she walked toward the circle of men around Nantze and finished the curate's words for him.

"They died," she whispered to the quiet room.

"Aye, lass," Palfrey cooed, stepped to her side, and patted her back affectionately. Wanting to change the subject quickly, he told her with a nod in Nantze's direction, "This here be the man I told ya 'bout. Mayhap he might stay a day or two and show us his craft and ability at the bellows. That is if'n ya agree ta him, of course. We men approve at present." The men, having said nothing so far, all began to shake their heads in agreement. A few even went so far as to toss out a word or two.

"Aye, Kate, a good man,"

"Be good at his craft, surely, if this here leg speaks ta the purpose," Pippen the Sweep announced with a wide grin as he held out Nantze's leg for her inspection.

Standing in front of Nantze and looking him over from head to toe, "Hmmph," she whispered with her arms locked protectively across her heart. Her first impression was that he was a might too handsome for a smithy.

His dark hair fell across a strong brow, his nose, which seemed chiseled, was thin and straight, and his brown eyes were softened by gentle lines, giving him an overall appearance of tender understanding, which didn't sit well with the girl. A man like that might try to use it to his advantage and take her forge. Beyond that he wore a working man's linen shirt, a brown leather vest, and tan trousers.

As she scrutinized him, he balanced on one leg in the center of the group of men, looking surprisingly strong amid the oddly assembled group of onlookers. "Lost yer leg I hear," she finally said, seeing his prosthetic leg being admired and held horizontally in the hands of Pippen the Sweep and his brother.

The question would have produced a howl of laughter from the men in any other circumstance, but since she had said it stoically and with a blank look in her bright eyes, they kept silent.

"Aye," Nantze nodded.

"And made legs fer yer mates?" she continued more kindly.

"Aye," Nantze choked out again, getting nervous under her sharp eye. Both of which were a magnificent shape and becoming to her face and figure. In fact, the combination of dark, braided hair, small, willowy wisps of fallen curls, and blue-green eyes was stunning; therefore, Nantze threw a look at the old codger, Palfrey, which said, "Repellent, indeed!"

The old man, reading Nantze's look correctly, smiled mischievously, and his eyebrows arched up with a quirky looking smile in return before pressing Katie for an answer. "What says ye, lass, ta a day or two?"

"Ya can take care of yerself, I suppose?" she asked Nantze.

"Aye, I can."

"And don't mind sleepin' in the loft above the forge?"

"Not at all."

Then she paused for a moment, thinking about what work needed to be done, and answered, "I'll give ya one week ta finish the church gate and a reasonable sum fer yer effort. After that, I'll make my decision," but then added sharply, "and I don't abide by excessive drinkin' nor carousin' either, mind!" she told him as she gazed around at all of the men holding a jar in their hands. "I'm a God fearin' gentlewoman!"

"Ya have my word," Nantze promised with a reassuring softness that emitted from his warm brown eyes, which made her feel as if maybe he could be trusted to keep it, making her breathe easier for a moment before thinking about something else she needed to nip in the bud before she agreed.

"And don't," she began, pointing a petite finger at his chest, "think this means I'm acceptin' ya because I'm not. I won't have no slovenly man workin' my father's forge, so I'll be reservin' my opinion until I see yer work." Then as an afterthought, she added harshly, "Nor am I gonna feed ya!" The gruffness of her words sounded cruel even in her own ears, so she added more gently and with a shake of her head, "I'm not up ta it just yet."

"I understand," Nantze cooed kindly and held out his hand as he would to a man to seal the deal, making most of the men gathered at the Yellow Sow hold their breath. One never quite knew what the little spitfire might do. Surprisingly, however, she exhaled, stretched out her own small hand, took ahold of Nantze's much larger one, and held on to it for much longer than was needed for a handshake.

In fact, it seemed to all the men who witnessed the event that the poor little thing was gathering some kind of strength from the exercise, and when she neither shook his hand nor let it go, Nantze, sensing her exhaustion, cupped his other strong, capable hand around her smaller one. "I won't disappoint ya. That I can promise!"

Shocked at his boldness, the rest of the men could do nothing more than hope Nantze hadn't taken too many liberties with the girl. Instead Katie just stood there quietly looking him in the eye, nodding her head, and breathing in and out in short raspy breaths as if the man was a soothing balm for her weary soul. After some few moments, she seemed to recollect that everyone was watching her and squeezed her hand out of his.

"Palfrey'll show ya the way!" she added, turned on her heel, and swiftly left the pub, leaving all of the men to silently stare after her departing form and wonder what had just taken place.

In the unnatural quiet of the bar, Palfrey offered, in his excited way, an explanation for the girl's transformation. "Miracle Nantze, indeed!" he spouted off as his twin brows rose in a hopeful arch. Many of the men shook their heads in agreement, remembering what the Londoner had said about the man during the Crimean War. What else could explain the taming of the shrew they wondered?

After Kate left and was presumably out of earshot, Kincaid suggested, "Well now, I says we celebrate with another pint!" He then grabbed up Nantze's leg from Pippen the Sweep, handed it back to the man who owned it, and made his way behind the bar. Those with a mite of ale still in the bottom of their jars swallowed what was left and followed him, making a boisterous show of their excitement at having so easily filled the position.

Beside himself with all that had transpired, Palfrey's bushy brows seemed to dance across his forehead in delight. In fact, he could not think of a better scenario than the one which had just taken place; therefore, moving across the room to sit in the brocade chair by the fire opposite Nantze as he put on his leg, Palfrey offered him a little advice. "If'n I was ya, I'd be up soon as that cock crows and stokin' the fire." Then thinking about what should be started first, he enlisted the curate to make a list of what things the Cinnies had left unfinished.

"I knowed they was workin' on the riggings and underpinnin' of O'Hare's curricle," someone offered.

"They were replacing a number of rungs on the Cathedral's fence and gate," the curate, Merriweather, said again. "And recall, what the girl said, 'You have one week to do it.'"

"They be mendin' one of my brooms," Pippen the Sweep added with an upraised arm. "Broke clean in two when I shoved it down old lady Crone's center chimney," he offered as an explanation for his broken equipment.

"More likely the old hag took it fer a lil' fly about when ya wasn't attendin'. The sly ol' witch!" Kincaid offered, making all the men nod in agreement that it was quite possible she had.

Smiling at their camaraderie and enjoying their company, Nantze promised to be at the forge bright and early and line out what he could make out from the supplies in the shop. "Come round though, each of ya, when time permits sometime after noon luncheon. I hope ta speak with Miss Kate in the mornin' and ask her ta point me in the direction she'd like me ta go."

"Well, now watch the lil' fire-sprite. She might suggest ya go ta the devil. One can never tell with that lass what she might say or do next!" offered Kincaid.

"Naw, not our Miracle Nantze! You just watch and sees what this here bloke can do!" offered Palfrey as he helped Nantze up out of his chair and led him towards the door once his leg was attached. "Better get settled in afore it gets too dark," he continued by way of explanation for their departure.

The truth was Palfrey had a few words to whisper in the man's ear privately concerning the girl; therefore, once they were settled in Nantze's hired rig with Palfrey at the reigns, the old man looked at the younger one and nodded, signaling his desire to tell the fellow something that should interest him.

"Nantze?"

"Aye, Palfrey?"

"I've a mind that ya should stay!"

"Well, now! I certainly am not in disagreement with ya, currently."

"Nor should ya be later if'n my lil' lass decides ta rain fire on ya, I hope?"

"Depends upon the heat, I suppose," Nantze told him in reply.

"The girl spits flames, surely, but she's only fearful of change.

She wants nothin' more than ta know she's safe. That's all any woman wants!" Palfrey popped off, hoping that Nantze had some understanding of the female sex.

"Perhaps that and ta be loved, I suppose," offer Nantze knowingly.

"I knewed ya were the bloke fer my girl the moment I clapped eyes on ya!" Palfrey smiled, his eyebrows dancing wildly across his brow. "I tell ya, the girl needs a body ta care fer. Every lass does!"

"Now, Palfrey, I'll admit I've always had a way with the womenfolk, but the truth of it is, once their eyes get an ogleful of my missin' limb or see me hobble 'round like a dog with three legs, they move on ta the next bloke."

"What of it?"

"There aren't any women waitin' at home hopin' fer some lame man ta come and rescue 'em!" he stated more plainly.

"That's just it, ya fool! She'd not accept no normal man what thinks too much of himself! She needs a man what needs her!"

"I'm not followin' ya?"

"That there lass could have any man in this county! Truth is, they probably would've already tried 'cept they were afraid of the girl's sharp tongue and her par's quick temper. Not ta mention Cinny. I tell ya he'd kill a fool afore lettin' a lad anywhere near Kate!" Here Palfrey seemed to stop and reflect. "Thin' is, Katie's never known anythin' but carin' fer those two, what with her mother dyin' after many a lost wee one. Now," Palfrey stopped mid-sentence to gather his thoughts, "I'm countin' on ya ta work another miracle!"

"And I can help, how?" Nantze asked, throwing his arms up in a sign of surrender.

Smiling, Palfrey went on, "Girl needs a reason ta live, Nantze! Just like those there blokes ya knewed in the war! The girl's lame. Not her leg but her heart!"

"And ya think I'm the man ta save her?"

"No, Nantze, I knewed ya be the man ta save her! I feel it. I just don't quite recollect yet how ta go about the savin'."

Seeing how very sincere old Palfrey was, Nantze smiled at the man and exclaimed, "I know nothin' about a loss of that kind."

"Damn it man, ya lost mates! Ya lost a limb. A part of yerself! That poor lass is no different. She's lost a part o' herself sure as ya have! She needs ta learn she's got a reason ta live. Needs a reason fer getting' herself up of a mornin'." Yanking out his discolored handkerchief and angrily swiping it across his eyes, he went on. "Now, ya listen ta an ol' man what's knowed this lass all her life, get her out ta the forge. Tell her yer needin' her ta tell ya what needs doin'. Say anythin', but somehow ya need ta save my girl!"

"Aye, but God does the savin' not me!"

"Well then, man o' God, start prayin' fer yer wife!"

Eyes protruding and wide, Nantze called out, "MY WIFE?"

"Aye, yer wife!" Palfrey told him as he jumped down from the rig when they arrived at the smithy shop. As Nantze clamored down from the bench and grabbed his gear, Palfrey unhooked the tired old nag, walked her to the empty stall in the barn, and then led Nantze into the open-air area that encompassed the forge. Inside it stood a single ladder that led to an upstairs loft.

As Palfrey pointed it out and the two looked up at it, a black skirt descended the ladder. When Katie saw the two, she offered a quick reason for her attendance in the loft. "Just tidin' up a bit." Palfrey, thinking that her admission was proof enough of his hypothesis, smiled at Nantze and shot him a knowing look. Seeing a passing glance, she added, "Hadn't been used in a while. Put clean sheets on the bed," she continued quietly, "and a quilt." Then thinking about the orange, tabby tomcat, she added, "Might find the cat curled up on yer bed. Notice he's been sleepin' up there."

Nantze, not knowing how to thank her without drawing too much attention to the kindness, only smiled. Palfrey, on the other hand, made a big show.

"Well now, Kate, that be right kind."

"Hmmph, it wasn't anythin' of the sort. I just dinna want it ta reflect bad upon my housekeepin' and ya know it. Ya ol' duffer!"

"Ya been talkin' ta the missus, I see! Ol' duffer, indeed!" Palfrey spit back, realizing too late that he'd made too much of her gesture. The girl had pride, and he for one was glad enough to see that she was able to set aside the ache in her heart to prepare the man's bed.

"Might ya take a minute ta show it ta him?" Palfrey asked, hoping that he might detain her long enough to get the two in company. She, however, shot him a look that told him she'd done all that she could for one outing and that he'd have to make sure the man was comfortable.

Palfrey, however, was not so easily derailed. He knew if he started spouting off something that offended her, the girl would have to intervene and perhaps even show the man around a little, so Palfrey called out as he ascended the ladder, "It's a small rickety place, this! Damn dusty, ta be sure."

"Shows what ya know, ya ol' duffer! Tis polished ta a shine!" Katie called out as she watched the old man go up to the loft with Nantze looking up at him as he held onto the ladder.

Turning around as he hung from one of the upper rungs, however, Palfrey turned and whispered down to Nantze in hopes of getting Kate involved, "Still rickety, says I!"

"Rickety, indeed! Pray how should ya know anythin' about it?"

"Mayhap I don't, but if yer leavin' me ta do the job, I 'spect I can introduce the place as I like, and what I says is, it's damn rickety! Besides that, I says it might be a damn nuisance fer a man with only one good leg ta traverse the horrors of this here ladder, but, I suppose, it canna be helped." Palfrey, feeling as if he'd hoodwinked the girl into showing Nantze around herself, waited for her irritation to overtake her pride, which, as Palfrey knew it would, took very little time.

It began with a huff as she placed her small hands upon her thin hips and was followed by her giving the man another earful. "What I says is, how Ivy's not maimed ya yet is a wonder since that jaw of yers never stops flappin' nonsense and talkin' bout things ya know nothin' about!" Before she knew it, she climbed up the ladder behind Nantze.

As Palfrey pulled back a curtain to let in more of the dimming light, Nantze wiggled himself through the opening to have a look at his new home and was surprised at how large the loft actually was. Even more surprising was the realization that the girl had followed behind him.

From where he stood at the entrance, he could see the entirety of the room. It spread before him some twenty-five-feet and at least ten feet from both sides of the entrance; however, even behind the ladder was another few feet.

The pitch of the thatched roof caused some enclosure, making him feel as if he was much too tall to stand upright unless in the center. Yet considering some of the places he had been forced to live and thrive in, he thought, as he looked about at the cozy nature of the loft, that he could manage quite well. There was a window straight ahead from the entrance and under it the bed was framed by two small wooden crates as tall as the bed itself, making them an ideal place to place a candle, lamp, or one's book for reading.

Looking around and settling his eyes on Katie, who had not actually entered the room but stood instead on one of the rungs of the ladder with only her head and upper body poking up into the room, he waited for the girl to speak.

"Ya can see behind ya here is where I keep my food goods."

Turning around, Nantze inspected the rest of the room. From the lowest rafters hung rows of onion, garlic, herbs and dried fruits. The floor, too, held baskets of food goods and gourds, and there were also graduating sized barrels for vinegar.

"Don't get any ideas about eatin' my dried fruits! I'll not have ya eat me out of house and home!"

"Wouldn't dream of doin' such a thing."

"Hmmph, I'll believe that when I see it, and don't think I won't check!"

"Just so!"

Thinking that the fool girl was going to scare away the new smithy before he ever had a chance to work the bellows and wanting to spark some sort of compassion in her heart for the man, Palfrey intervened. "Look here!" he spouted off as he hopped energetically around the room before picking up a lamp upon one of the bedside crates and setting it down on a nearby toiletry stand. "Ya've yer own washbasin and mirror fer shavin'. I doubt ya saw that in the war."

"I saw many things less inviting, ta be sure!"

Palfrey, seeing that he was still looking at Katie, added, "I suppose ya have. Damn horrible travesty, war is!"

Not being able to disagree, Nantze shook his head in agreement. "I should never like ta see it again in my lifetime."

Then when neither man spoke, Katie added to the conversation. "I suppose it was not too different from what I happened upon," she offered in a whisper as the image of her father and brother's dead bodies entered her mind again. Hoping Nantze might be able to prove his mettle with the girl, Palfrey did something he very rarely did. He waited to see if the girl would elaborate without any nudging from him.

"I can only think that somethin' must have spooked the horse ta make it bolt. There is no other reason why they should have taken that bend in the road at such speeds as would throw 'em out of the wagon and inta the wall."

Nantze waited quietly for her to go on, his eyes attempting to encourage her to keep talking. In contrast, had anyone looked at the old man, they'd have seen his eyes pop open with fright as he recalled what he'd seen the morning the Cinnies died. Believing the horse must have seen the same caped rider he'd witnessed that morning and been spooked by it and thinking that he would be as daft as his wife claimed him to be if he mentioned what he'd seen, he said nothing, hoping that, perhaps, Nantze would be able to work another miracle on the girl and get her to release the sorrow that she'd bound to her chest like a blanket.

"I don't suppose what ya saw was much different," Nantze answered quietly as he held out his hand, inviting her to come out of the ladder well and enter the room to stand beside him.

"I cannna release the damn plaguey sight!" she whispered. Seeing his offered hand, she paused, looked into his warm brown eyes, and noticeably quaked before nodding her head a few times to steady her emotions. Wanting very much to calm her, Nantze, with his arm outstretched toward her, waited patiently for her to accept it.

Staring at his proffered support and breathing deeply numerous times in succession, she finally reached out and gingerly took his hand. Waiting until she was steady and standing next to him, he slowly released his hold on her, but her fingers lingered slightly, making him feel that she deeply wanted to have someone to comfort her. This truth washed over his heart like a tidal wave, and he wondered if Palfrey hadn't been divinely inspired when the old man had told him to start praying for his wife.

After such a tender moment, Nantze was careful to speak soothingly. "Aye, that'll take some time, I think." His voice, being uncommonly deep, settled the girl, and she went on.

"I canna sleep. I just keep seein' their broken bodies lyin' there." Her voice was almost unrecognizably soft and childlike. Her body, too, dwarfed and exhausted, shifted to stand closer to Nantze. He, being a tall man, made Kate look all the more vulnerable.

"Probably best ta wear yerself out. You work the bellows?"

"I do. Par never liked me ta do it over much. 'It's not work,' he said, 'fer the gentler sex,' but on some occasions when there was a lot ta do, he'd have me stoke the fire or organize his work bench."

"Yer welcome ta work it in the mornin' if ya like, but like he said, not over much. I found though, when I was recoverin' from my wounds, that it does a body good ta have some task ta perform. It redirects the mind."

"I might do that. Lord knows I've precious little ta occupy my thoughts."

"I know that good and well. I saw more cracked ceilings than I ever hope ta see again. Got so sick of lookin' at nothin' I tore myself out of the bed one day like it was hell itself!" Nantze told her with a faraway look in his gentle brown eyes. In a moment he added, "It was a hell! A hopeless pit I felt stuck in. I promised myself I'd never get back in that bed, and I didn't. Slept in a chair, hobbled on crutches, then I started thinkin' on how ta get on with the work of livin'! I thought hard on the verse that said, 'Let the dead bury the dead. You follow Me.' I took it ta mean I was alive, and it was time fer me ta start figurin' out why!"

"What'd ya learn?"

"That there was a whole lot more ta livin' than bein' alive!"

"What'd ya mean?"

"I mean there is a difference between being alive and havin' somethin' ta live fer!" Nantze told her in a whisper as he pushed back a stray strand of her hair. "We canna go back! No matter how we wish we could! We can only find the value in the life we have now, Kate. That takes a bit o' time, searchin', and a whole lot of forgivin' yerself fer not havin' died too!"

"Aye," she cried, tears coming to her eyes. "That's the puzzle I canna make out! Why should I be livin' and the rest of my family in the ground?"

"No, Kate!" he began firmly, surprising her so much so that she snapped her eyes to look at him. "Not in the ground!" His voice was laced with such strength and charged with such passion, she found herself nodding in understanding. "God does not suffer His loved ones ta rot. Right? Dinna Paul say, 'absent from the body is present with the Lord?'"

"He did!"

"Didn't he also say, 'fer me ta live is Christ?'"

"Yes, but he said, 'ta die is gain,'" she answered weakly, making her comment seem more like an enigma she hoped he'd explain, which, of course, he did.

"Yer not dead yet, are ya?" he asked in a very pointed whisper. After she answered the obvious question with a small shake of her head, he added, "Then live ta Christ!"

"How?" she asked, her eyes filled with tears.

"God made time fer mankind! He surely don't need it, now does He?"

"I suppose not."

"You know He don't. He made it fer us. Each day has enough troubles of its own. So don't go worryin' about how you'll make it through tomorrow. Have faith in God and His Son Jesus Christ. Love yer fellow man as He commands. This pleases the Lord.

After that, set yerself ta task. Divide yer day into sections. Pray. Read God's word. Do yer chores. Sew. Eat. Sleep. One day at a time, lass. Trust God has a plan fer ya. That's the way." After a pause in which neither spoke but both felt emotionally drained, Nantze finally asked, "Might ya come ta the forge in the mornin' even if ya don't work? Ya can tell me where ta start first, eh? Or if ya rather, ya could maybe organize the work and the bench?"

She didn't answer but nodded that she'd come. When the conversation seemed to be at an end, Palfrey, who'd crouched down out of the way, came out from his corner, "There now, let's be off with ya ta bed, hmm, Kate?"

Looking up at him, Katie nodded her head and followed Palfrey's lead; however, once she got to the opening in the floor and gone down a few rungs on the ladder to where only her doe-eyed face was left to Nantze's view, she called out to him, "This don't mean I'll let ya stay!"

Smiling at her fighting spirit but sad that she'd already replaced the guard-like shield around her heart, Nantze nodded that he understood. "You just come round in the mornin', lass, so ya can give me yer instructions and inspect my work!"

Saying nothing but offering a weak nod, Katie went with Palfrey. Her dog, who had waited at the foot of the ladder, followed the pair out of the shop. Allowing herself to be led back up to the house, Katie curled up in her father's large chair by the hearth, and Palfrey pulled a blanket around her. "Now, get ya before the fire and protect yer mistress, ya wiry hound," he told the dog, who'd followed the pair into the house. Doing as he was told, the dog curled up at the foot of her chair. Adding another log to the fire, Palfrey patted the mutt on the head, stood, kissed Kate on the forehead, and showed himself out.

The old man, however, had not even made it out the door before he was required to fish out his handkerchief and mop the moisture from his wooly eyes. He'd not felt so hopeful in weeks. In fact, now that Miracle Nantze was come and introduced to Kate, Palfrey was desirous of mending the mischief and mayhem left behind by the grim rider who'd started this whole horrid affair, so he set his mind to the task of which way would be best to worm Nantze into the lady's affection. However, by the time he'd gotten home to Ivy and his own bed, he'd still not hit upon a scheme.

Nantze, on the other hand, mulled over Palfrey's insane talk as he took off his leg and prepared himself for bed. "Pray fer my wife, indeed! He is an ol' duffer!" he scoffed, thinking about what the old man had said. Still he did have to admit she was a pretty little thing, but Nantze had come following employment not looking to get himself hitched.

He didn't like the idea of anyone thinking he had designs to gain the smithy by such means, and reminded himself that he would have to tread very lightly around the subject of Katie Christison. "Who am I kiddin'? I'll have to tread lightly around Kate, period!" he muttered as he climbed in between the fresh sheets of the comfortable bed she'd made up for him.

∞ ∞ ∞

Chapter Four

The following morning, Nantze was up with the light. He'd eaten a pathetic gruel, and stood sipping his tea as he hobbled round the forge, attempting to familiarize himself with the materials and work stations. Off in the corner stood Pippen the Sweep's beheaded broom. That was an easy fix, so as soon as his fire was hot, he reattached the spindly wire broom. He did, however, make some little twists in the wrought iron handle, which allowed for a man to wield it with more grip. It was a design of his own, which he particularly liked. It gave the handle a good weight, and it felt good in his hands.

Next seeing many of the iron fencing rods in a pile ready to be formed, Nantze inspected the previous work, admired the artistry, and set to copy its exact likeness. By the time Katie wandered out to the forge dressed in a tattered old work gown and leather apron, Nantze had made two such rods for the fence and had other pieces softening in the fire.

Inspecting them and not being able to tell which had been created prior to his coming, Katie nodded her approval of the few he'd finished. Then taking down a clipped-board from a nearby nail in one of the roughhewn wooden beams of the forge, she told Nantze, "The Cathedral ordered two-hundred and eighty-five such rods."

"How many are finished there?"

After a few moments counting and her marking the number on the list, Katie responded, "Over half."

Doing some quick mental math, Nantze spouted off, "Should be able ta have those done by mid-week, surely." Then wondering how the Cinnies had been in the habit of collecting funds, he asked, "How do ya wanna go about collecting payment? Need I say anythin'?"

"No, my par always made the men pay me. Said he had no mind fer figurin' out sums, and they all believed him. Wasn't true, of course." Not having anything else to say, Kate moved over to the bellows and opened and closed the beastie lungs of the contraption for Nantze as he gathered up another armload of iron rods for the fence and moved them closer to the forge.

The labor seemed to help the girl. Soon, like Nantze, sweat dripped from her face, and she swiped it away with a delicate handkerchief she stored in the gown-length, leather apron she wore secured across her front side. Her apron, however, had a small flap that also pressed across her rump to keep her skirt pasted to her legs and away from any stray flame. Before too terribly long, a stripe of soot decorated the bridge of her nose, and her massive array of hair had some tiny tendrils that had fallen out of their confinement and curled about her ears and the nape of her slim neck. Just looking at her made Nantze's heart lurch.

Knowing the Turks believed in the health benefits of dripping sweat, Nantze thought it might release some of the girl's pent up angst and get her muscles relaxed through over use. It would certainly help her sleep at night. However, when noon rolled around the two broke to take their separate meals, Nantze recalled his instructions to the men he'd met last night and went to enlighten Kate. "I expect some men what's waitin' on their jobs ta get done will come round after they've supped. Mayhap ya'd like ta tidy up afore they get here."

Looking down at her filthy hands and feeling the wet fabric of her oldest dress sticking to her skin, she nodded, went to the pump to fill a bucket, and did not return until she heard the dog bark, signaling that they had visitors.

Of course, the first to arrive was Palfrey. He'd been chomping at his reserve all morning long, but wanting to give Nantze an opportunity to work a miracle, he paced incessantly across the rug before the fireplace, making his wife finally exclaim, "Ya damn duffer! Get yerself off would ya, afore ya wear a hole clean through the only floor coverin' I've got ta keep out the cold."

"Pssh, woman, let a man be! My puzzler be puzzlin' on how ta get that fiery lil' lass attached ta this new man Nantze what's come afore the fool girl runs him off."

"Don't ya go spreadin' yer fool ideas around like Christmas candy and interferin' where ya have no cause."

"Shows what ya know! I tell ya, that girl'll follow after the pair of Cinnies if'n she's got naught ta occupy her, but ya give the girl a chit or two, and she'll have reason ta live on."

"As lil' as she is, she'd more likely follow her mother's method ta the grave. Sides, she canna very well marry bein' in her black skirts another five months or more."

"Aye! She'll never forsake what's due her father's memory. I know that very well! Still must be some way?"

"Perhaps ya aught let him first stamp out his week. Might find out he ain't got the meddle fer a girl with a tongue as sharp as a needle's end nor an arm what can wield a hammer fer hours on end."

"Blah! The man's got meddle enough and arms as big as most men's legs!" he gaped at her with a wave of his hand as if to ask who the duffer was now. However, when the clock on the fireplace mantle chimed, signifying the noon hour, having been distracted by the conversation, the old man jumped at the sound, and in response to his surprise, the two furry lines on his brow began to gyrate, making them look like they were moving across his forehead. "Well, now. That be my sign. Suppose I'll just ramble 'round ta see how the boy's made out this mornin'."

Seeing Palfrey as the spry, spindly man came into the yard, Nantze hobbled over to see if his new friend would do him a favor. "Since I am ta stay a week, I need ta return that rented nag and cart and send a letter not ta give up my room. I told Wilmarth, he owns the forge there in Lancaster, that I had some personal business in Carlisle that might take me some few days ta put in order. Might ya help me? I canna walk the distance back on this bum leg. Ya think ya could send this letter and return the cart?"

"I've naught ta do when I leave here. 'Sider the work done!"

Smiling at him, Nantze replied, "I suppose then ya'd let me get yer ale later at the Sow?"

"I'll not only let ya get it, I'll come round ta fetch ya."

"I hope yer bringin' a rig?" Nantze joked, making a big show of his worst wobbling walk. "Otherwise I'll be walkin' like this fer a week straight."

Palfrey liked the pantomime so well his twin caterpillar brows raised with a hoot of laughter, and he answered, "I can do that." Expecting that to be his answer about the cart, Nantze was surprised when the old man proceeded to walk around the yard aping the same wobbly sort of movements Nantze had demonstrated a moment ago, and the two shared another chuckle.

As Nantze bit off a chunk of bread and washed it down with tea, he watched as some of the other men began to filter into the yard and offer their greetings. Having come to see if Nantze was genuinely capable, a group of them rushed into the shop to see his progress, while Kate sat inconspicuously upon the porch with her dog at her feet.

Pippen the Sweep, after seeing his restored broom, offered his praise first. "Well, I'd not have thought to add that twist there, but I tell ya it gives it a good weight and grip, now don't it?"

"Glad ya like the improvement! I find that type of broom handle sweeps better because ya can get yer hands around it fer a proper shove and pull like what's needed fer a chimney sweep."

"Let me get a look at it?" Kincaid asked, holding out his hand for the broom. After examining it a moment or two, the man laughed. "Let's see that ol' witch Crone break this thin' with another fly about. I tell ya it canna be done!" With that the group of men laughed.

The curate, more anxious than anyone, looked at the pile

of decorated iron fence rods. "Now which are yours and which belong to the Cinnies?"

"Yer guess would be as good as mine," Nantze began but then remembered something. "Wait… wait…" he added then hobbled around to the rod he'd used as a sample and held it up. "This one was made by the Cinnies fer certain. I used it ta make the others."

Taking up the original and looking at the rest in the pile, the curate was unable to see any differences in craftsmanship. "Well now, I proclaim this to be very fine work!"

"And that from the man o' God!" Palfrey offered to all those who had come to see Nantze's work. Then poking his bony elbow into Nantze's side and giving him a wink, he added, "Sounds like we got a man we can all agree on so far." With that the men all shook their heads positively.

"But we still need to see him set the bars to the fence. That'll be the final test, I think?" the curate offered, and all the men agreed that they would all save their opinion until that time.

"Very well," answered Palfrey. "We all agrees then that he'll have the fence done by the end of the week, and everyone can cast their vote about makin' him the new smithy then."

"What about the fire-sprite? Ya gonna give the girl a vote?" one of the men whispered and nodded his head toward the porch where she sat.

"I've my own plans fer her. Ya just leave the lass ta me," Palfrey told the men. "And don't none of ya worry about that. Ya just keep prayin' the girl won't give inta despair or scare away our man Miracle Nantze, here!"

"Gladly!" they all answered in unison, making the merry little band of men feel as if they were all of one accord for the girl's good.

"Well then men, I've a lot ta finish up," Nantze began as he started moving around to the forge and working the bellows. "Pippen the Sweep, go on up ta the house and pay the boss!" Nantze added, making sure all the men knew he didn't view himself as in charge.

"Aye, can someone come with me?" he asked, balancing the

weight of the new handle in his hands and making all the men howl with laughter.

"Yer man enough, I think!" Kincaid offered with a small shove.

Turning back to Nantze, Pippen asked, "Will ya do this ta all my brooms?"

"Of course, just tell Kate, there. She'll give ya yer price."

A look of sudden fear gripped the man, "Talk ta her? She might likely rail me!" he told the men as he dipped into his trouser pocket for his purse and walked up to the house to pay the girl.

He didn't know what to say to her. She always muddled up his words in his head. There wasn't a girl as beautiful to his way of thinking, nor one as able to take a man's insides and turn them to gruel. When he walked up, she was sitting on the porch in a clean black dress. She looked serene enough, Pippin thought to himself, but with Kate one could never be too sure.

Having to swallow his fear before he could open his mouth, the gawky looking young man wiped his sweaty palms on his trousers and slicked his hair down to prepare himself. "Now what do ya say ta this, Kate?" he asked nervously as he showed off his fixed broom. "I like the weight and feel so much, I told Nantze, I'd like him ta do it ta all my brooms." Here the man hawed a little then continued, "Well, that is, if'n it ain't ginna put a hole in my purse."

Having known the man her whole life and knowing how horribly he struggled when talking to girls, she nodded politely and spoke. "If'n all he's doin' is heatin' em up ta add the twist, I should think tuppence should cover it. You'll have ta wait a piece afore he can get ta 'em. Gotta finish the Cathedral fence first. Aught be done with the rods by mid-week, I suppose, and it'll take most of the rest of his week ta put the rods on the frame and set them."

"Mayhap ya might let him stay a might longer," he offered as he handed her his coin. Kate nodded at him as she stretched out her arm; however, she did not reply.

She hadn't said anything to Nantze this morning, but when she awoke at dawn and heard the familiar ping of the hammer, she'd nuzzled down deeper into the cushions of her father's over-sized chair, forgetting her loss entirely. Later when the dog nudged her and began to whine to go outside, the remembrance of their deaths slapped her conscious thoughts with a horrific blow and flashed the scene of their maimed bodies across her mind-screen, squeezing another notch in the tourniquet surrounding her heart and making her fear she would not be able to even have the man finish out the week so difficult were the memories he exposed.

∞ ∞ ∞

Chapter Five

Later that evening, after Nantze had an opportunity to finish up his work in the forge and let the fire burn down to embers, he grabbed the bar of soap and the towel kept by the door and wobbled himself over to the pump to clean up. The well was under a small wall-less hut (much like the forge) with a little thatched roof to keep the rain and sun from decaying the working mechanisms of the pump. It also offered a bit of protection for Kate as she washed clothes and preserved foods. From the roughhewn boards hung Kate's wash basin, outdoor canning supplies, kettles and the like. As Nantze looked around, he realized it felt homey, comfortable. Like holding Kate's hand, it just felt right.

Dismissing such thoughts and grabbing up a bucket from a peg, Nantze began to pump water into it while intermediately shoving his hands in the cool water and splashing it in his face and around his head and neck. Next, he lathered up and began to wash away the day's grime. His shirt, soaked with sweat and dirt, needed washing. It came off and was plunged into the sudsy water then used as a cloth to finish washing his chest, head, and under his arms. After that, it went back in the bucket again, and Nantze began to scour it with the soap.

"There's a washboard right there ta yer left hangin' on that peg."

"Kate!" Nantze, being startled and bare chested, jumped and turned around to face the tiny woman curled up on a chair on the porch. As he spun around to face her, he pulled his wet shirt up to his chin and groaned. Moving at such uncharacteristic speeds for a man with only one leg, he wobbled ungracefully and nearly fell as he whirled about. It was too late though, she'd seen what he didn't want her to.

"So it's not just yer leg that's injured, I see. What's all those other scars? Where'd they come from?"

Exhaling, he answered. "Scraps of whatever came flyin' at me, I suppose, wood and bone. They look like the very devil but don't hurt much." After a small pause, it was obvious Kate was thinking because she changed the subject in her blunt way.

"I've not worked the bellows in a while, ya won't tell the men will ya? Par never liked the idea of me workin' over much. It's hot work fer a woman, but it gives me somethin' ta do!"

"Aye, it's hot work fer a man!" he answered, looking at the concern in her eyes. "But I'll keep it ta myself, and if'n you'll not mention my wounds, I'd appreciate that, too. Won't do those men any good knowin' I'm all beat up. It makes people pity ya, and I hate the look of pity in a man's eyes directed at me. It's a damn cruel emotion!"

"Fair enough. Mind, I don't want yer pity either," she told him rather coldly, considering all that had passed between them so far. However, her next words shed a bright light, making him understand her resentment. "Besides, it looks like I need ya, or so says all the men."

His voice, when he spoke, held the same gentle energy of correction he'd used last night. "They're doin' exactly what yer par and brother would want them ta do. So don't dishonor them by resentin' their care and affection fer ya."

Even from where he stood, he could see her tears. "I know. I'm just not ready."

"They're good men, Kate."

Pulling herself up out of the chair, she sputtered more harshly,

"I suppose you'll go ta the Sow ta get yer supper?" She knew she'd told him she wasn't going to feed him, but now that she realized he was going to leave, she felt empty.

"Aye, Palfrey's comin' round ta fetch me. Can't go walkin' that far on this bum leg, nor can I survive on what I can make fer myself!" Nantze offered, slapping his leg for emphasis and trying to make her see she had a lot to be thankful for. Then the two became quiet again.

"Yer a good worker!" Katie's whisper was angelic, which was a stark contrast to her earlier speech and all the hard lines etched across her countenance in the dimming light.

"Aye, ya are too. Ya comin' round ta help me in the mornin'?"

"Aye, I'll come. Got nothin' else worth doin' when I get up."

"Come, I need yer help and yer instructions! You know who needs what and are better able ta tell me what's most important," Nantze told her somewhat dishonestly. He'd worked forges by himself for most of his life. The Lord knew he could work the smithy on his own. She, however, didn't need to know that at present. The girl, having nothing to look forward to and nothing to do, needed the work more than he needed the help.

Seeing that he was going and having nothing else she might say without crying, Kate went in the house. Her faithful hound followed behind her, leaving the cat with little more to do than look up at Nantze and watch him finish up his toiletry.

Done with his washing and wringing out the wet things, Nantze teetered to the clothes line and slapped his linen shirt across it before pulling more water into the bucket and taking it up to the loft to finish cleaning up and changing for the pub. Palfrey would be along soon.

Seeing Kate go into the house so solemnly, Nantze almost felt like he was betraying the girl. Still there was only so much he could do, and more than anything else, he told himself, "A man's got ta eat!"

From inside the cottage, Kate watched him hobble back to the forge and had to smile at the cat, who, trotting behind him, pranced around all the splotches of water that spilled out because of Nantze's lopsided walk. Shaking her head, she whispered, "Judas!" When the dog lifted his head and looked at her in a questioning way, she added, "The cat has betrayed us!" Never having really cared over much for the lazy tom, the dog lowered his big head back down upon his outstretched paws and sighed, signifying the cat's wily ways had, in his opinion, shown an inconstancy for years.

Once in the loft, Nantze began to consider his options and attempt to dispel the burden he felt for the girl. When he'd first seen Hutchins and Cummings at the station, he'd thought his interview in Carlisle was Godly intervention to get a better pay out of the railroad. However, now that he'd met Palfrey and Kate, he wasn't so sure that God wasn't telling him he needed to stay here. "A man could make a decent wage workin' fer the railroad if'n he played his cards right!" he told himself as he removed his leg and was surprised when the large orange tomcat meowed in return.

He'd been equally surprised when the dumb thing came and curled up on the bed with him the night before. Not having been used to having an animal about, he kicked at it and flung it off the bed before it had time to circle round and find a good spot. Undaunted, the furry beast made his way back up on the bed so many times during the night that Nantze eventually gave up trying to aim at it with his one good leg, and both of them finally got some sleep.

As he thought about his possibilities, an image of Katie flashed across his mind. "Mayhap I should just take my time afore I make any rash decisions," he told himself as he detached his leg, pulled off his dirty trousers, and hung them on a peg to air out before pulling a clean shirt over his head. "Won't do no good chasin' after money if'n God has a different plan!" This idea evidently set well with the cat, too, because in an instant, he was purring and rubbing his furry head against Nantze's metal leg, which he'd propped up beside the wash basin.

"What have I got myself into?" Picking up his fake leg, he flung the cat off and the beast went whizzing helter-skelter across the wood floor. After this new amusement, Nantze grabbed up a crutch to keep himself balanced and went to his duffel bag to fish out a brush and comb.

The wash basin sat atop a wooden stand, which had a mirror screwed into two arms that came up off the backside of the stand. Under the basin were two shelves. One held towels. The other was empty. Nantze unloaded his supplies and placed them there.

Looking at himself in the mirror, he decided to leave the stubble on his face. It made no real difference whether he kept it or not. No one here cared if he was clean shaven. Besides that, he was tired, and he'd have to go down and fetch more water for the procedure since he'd already used the water he brought with him.

His crutches stood beside the stand, and a small stool sat in front of it. Sitting down, he cleansed and pampered his stump by rubbing it down with salve. Looking over at his metal leg, he decided, "I'll just leave that behind!" However, it wasn't long before the cat was back and rubbing against it.

Watching the furry orange and white tom scratch against his fake leg, he sighed. "Just do the job ya've come ta do and don't go worryin' about the girl or what some of the men might think." As he looked at himself in the mirror, he pulled a brush through his thick brown hair, and said a prayer to the Almighty. "I hope ya know what yer doin', Lord."

"Oy, there Nantze!" Palfrey called out from the bottom of the ladder. "It's time ya got some grub!"

"Just comin'!" Then because he could, Nantze picked up his leg again and pushed the cat off with a swift swipe, tossing it airborne. Not one to go quietly, the cat's angry protest could be heard below.

"Well now, glad ta see yer gettin' on so well with the cat!" Palfrey called up when he heard the tom.

"Yes, like oil and water!" Handing down his crutches, facing forwards, and hopping down one rung at a time as he held onto the opening in the floor, Nantze made his way down to the forge.

"Givin' the stump a rest?"

"Aye, it's always good ta give it a good airin'." Chuckling, he added, "Well, it and the cat."

"So that was the ol' tom's complaint, was it? Ya gave it a wee bit of a swing, I suppose?"

"Thinks my leg is his new scratchin' post." Then grinning, he added, "I tell ya, that foot unit comes in quite handy at times! Many uses, it has, and that's a fact!"

As they spoke the old tom cat jumped down into the forge to escort Nantze to the waiting rig, and as an example of his true constancy and affection began to rub against his crutches, causing both of them to howl with laughter, and Nantze to give it another little shove.

Still laughing, the men loaded up and drove to the Sow amid a lively conversation about Nantze's first day working the bellows. In fact, it was the same conversation the men at the Sow were conducting upon their arrival.

"Where's yer leg, man?" Kincaid asked, his eyes bobbling wide when Nantze hobbled in on his crutches.

"Have ya gone and hurt yerself already, and it only been the first day?" Pippen the Sweep asked, fearful Nantze wouldn't be able to finish the work on his brooms.

"Or did that little fire-sprite shoot arrows at ya?" his brother asked, jabbing at his twin with his elbow.

"No worries about Kate and me. We get on well enough." Nantze told the men.

"Now, that would be a miracle! Ya just wait till she's feelin' more like herself."

"Aye, Death shook the wind from her sails, he did."

"She'll rightin' up!" Palfrey parried and held out his mug for a fill.

"Ya work yer leg raw?" Kincaid asked rather quietly, concern edged in his voice as he pulled on the keg and filled Palfrey's glass.

"Na, just good ta let it get some air of an evening. I'll take a pint and a meal." Leaning on his crutches at the bar, Nantze took stock of the men milling about. They were a hardworking set.

Nudging Palfrey, "Will ya carry that tray ta the table there fer me?" Nodding that he would, Nantze carted himself over to the stuffed chairs at the fire, took a seat, and put his crutches upon the floor. Once Palfrey brought over the tray, Nantze bowed his head respectfully, voiced a silent prayer, and took to his meal like one ravenous.

"Ya needn't fall on it with such lust man! It's only stew," Palfrey suggested as he took the chair beside him.

"I dinna eat much of a lunch." Nantze paused, chewed, and shoved in another spoonful. "Just a bite of bread and butter and a lil' cheese." This dialog was followed with the same routine as Nantze chewed, swallowed, and reloaded almost as one famished. "I'm about ta die eatin' my own grub. The shop I've been workin' fer feeds me like a king, so I'm used ta eatin' three decent meals a day. I tell ya, Wilmarth's wife, Wilmarth is the owner of the forge, makes us a decent spread fer every meal." Here he paused before filling his mouth again. "Course, if'n I take the railroad job, I'll have ta find myself a new place," Nantze began, then shook his head at his own ignorance. That was a piece of information he wasn't going to let loose of.

"The railroad!" Palfrey began in a rushed whisper as he leaned in closer to Nantze. His eyebrows, being fully offended by such talk, lowered in an angry scowl. "Those blokes offerin' fer ya?"

Not being able to get away from telling the man now that he'd gone and opened his fool mouth, Nantze whispered back in hushed tones too low for the rest of the men to hear. "Aye, they caught me in the station on my way here. Told 'em I'd be gone a few days, but that I'd think it over if they offered me an agreeable wage, which of course they've not done."

"Let's not let on about their offer just yet. Don't wanna ruin yer chances with the girl."

"Just because yer wantin' me ta help her, doesn't mean she'll accept it from me. She's proud."

"Aye, that she is! But the truth is, ya've made more headway with the girl than any of us blokes!" Palfrey added, thinking of how much she'd opened up to him so far. Shaking his head as he watched Nantze shovel in another loaded mouthful of stew, Palfrey thought about the railroad. Bending closer to Nantze so that only he could hear him, the old man added, "Just the same, we'll keep that lil' secret under our hats, hmm?"

"I wasn't goin' ta tell ya about it. Just happened ta slip out."

"Well, we'll not talk of it again. Especially not here. Won't do the men any good if they think yer not serious about the offer." Swigging again from his glass, Palfrey's eyebrows were up in arms and squirming, making Nantze believe he was offended by the very idea of him considering any other option; therefore, he answered back in harried low tones.

"Now wait a minute, I never said I wasn't serious about workin' the forge here. I'm greatly interested," Nantze whispered back. "I just want ta keep my options open. We don't even know if Kate plans on keepin' me, and I have ta think of my future, ya know. A man like me can't work forever."

"Well, I canna argue about that, now can I?" he answered more kindly, making his eyebrows relax their offended stance.

"Not if ya plan ta make a case, no! There's nothin' wrong with me havin' options."

After this small dialog and once Nantze had finished his meal, the two joined the conversation going on around them, and as the men did every night, they discussed the details of the day. The first topic, of course, was how Nantze made out.

"Did you happen to finish the posts for the cathedral?" the curate asked after seeking out Nantze. His appearance at the Sow was a noteworthy one, considering he was not a regular there. However, now that the gate was again underway, he was curious about its progress.

"Now, I'll admit I'm as hard a worker as any, but I rather doubt even the Cinnies working all day together on those slats could have had the job done by tonight." Then considering putting the fence in the ground, Nantze added out loud to the group, "I'll be needin' a horse and cart when I'm done ta carry the sections ta the church fer hangin', and try as I might, I canna lift 'em on my own. I'll be needin' some help to keep myself from toppling over. Is there a young man I might hire fer the job?" As Nantze spoke, many of the men offered their carts and even their help. "Alright, then, I'll let ya know when I'm ready. Whoever is able can come 'round and give me a hand."

Then turning to the man of God, Nantze added, "I'll prepare a section of fencing, so ya can get the holes dug fer the posts. Can't have the work done by week's end if'n they don't hire some lads ta prep the grounds."

"Very well, I'll come around tomorrow for it," the curate told him after some few moments. "Glad you mentioned it. I'd not given it any thought."

"Come after ya've supped. That'll give me time ta finish it up. Should keep the boys busy fer some few days. Make sure they sink the section in the holes they dig, mind, or it'll all be fer naught."

"Well now, Nantze, sounds like ya had a right full day!" Kincaid offered as he picked up the tray and wiped down the table.

"I'll not argue about that, that's fer certain. Put Palfrey's ale there on my tab," he offered as he poked a thumb in the man's directions. "The ol' codger took my rented nag back fer me today."

"Now that was right kind!" Kincaid, looking at Palfrey, offered.

"I thought so, too. I had no desire ta stumble my way back in any case. It's a damn nuisance bein' lame."

Kincaid, seeing his point, nodded his agreement.

Palfrey, on the other hand, trying to reconfigure the railroad's job offer into his scheme to keep Nantze in Carlisle, thought more about how to get Kate attached to the man. "Mayhap, she might be afraid ta lose such a good worker as he is," he thought to himself, "if'n she knew the railroad had plans to snatch him away." With all this hard thinking, Palfrey's eyebrows paced back and forth across his brow in obvious thought.

Before long, Nantze and Palfrey said their good-byes, loaded themselves on the hard cart bench, and trotted home. Having had time to think things through and wanting Nantze to see the benefits of accepting the job, Palfrey decided it would be in his best interest to highlight the advantages of working in Carlisle.

"Well now, Nantze, seems as if ya fit right in. Mayhap like ya were born here. The men have takin' quite an uncommon likin' ta ya."

"I'll admit I dinna expect such friendly fellows. Kincaid I like."

Palfrey, playing at being offended, said, "What? Ya wound me, man!"

At that Nantze jabbed the old man in the ribs. "Yer not of their mien."

"There yer right. I am a man of great intellectual auspiciousness," Palfrey told him with a tip of his hat and an ear to ear grin, exposing his missing teeth.

Caught off guard by such high-winded talk, Nantze could only laugh at the old man.

"I doubt ya'd be so entertained workin' like a dog fer the railroad!"

"I am sure yer right about that, but a man can make a good livin' at it."

"Money does make the world go 'round, as they says, but it also makes fer a bit o' lonely life. A man needs mates!" Almost adding, "and a mate," to the end of his statement, Palfrey checked himself. "No sense scaring the man away with such talk," he reminded himself. Although it was obvious to him that Nantze was the perfect man to temper Kate's fire, Nantze didn't know it yet. More importantly, Kate didn't know it, and Palfrey knew he'd be a fool to try to tell it to either one of them.

Seeing that Palfrey was trying to sell him on all the advantages of the job, Nantze just nodded his head and put aside the idea until he could think about it properly. The decision was a big one, and he wanted to make sure he took his time weighing out the good and bad of both jobs. As it was, it was late, and he was more tired than he thought he should be.

Once back at the shop, the two men sat a moment. "Just want ya ta make sure ya equal in more than an income. A man's got ta have his health fer the kind o' job ya do."

"There is no denyin' that!" Nantze answered. Gathering up his crutches, he tumbled down from the cart, waving to Palfrey as he went. Seeing no lights on in the house, he assumed Kate had already gone to bed.

He certainly felt for the girl, but apart from that he had no idea how to go about accomplishing what Palfrey hoped for. "The crazy ol' man!" Nantze muttered to himself with a smile as he hobbled over to the well. "Pray fer yer wife! What kind of talk is that?" he muttered again when Kate's dog came rambling over to him and whined. "Well boy?" he asked as he scratched the dog behind his ears. "What ya doin' out here?" Looking up at the porch, he thought he saw Kate curled up on a chair. Grabbing up his crutches and placing them under his arms, he wobbled his tired body over to get a better view.

"Kate," he whispered. "Kate!" he said again but still received no answer. Hobbling up the few steps, Nantze moved to stand over her. The dog, too, went up on the porch and lie down at her feet. Curled up in the chair next to her was the fat, old tom. Hearing him make a racket as he fumbled with his crutches on the porch, the cat stretched out and yawned. After a few moments interlude, Nantze tried again. When she didn't move, he shook her shoulders slightly until she brushed his hand away with a slap. "Kate, ya need ta go in the house!"

"Aye, and ya can go ta the devil!" she answered back, and cuddled down into a blanket she had tucked up under her chin. Chuckling at her quick-witted comeback, Nantze took stock of the girl in the low moonlight. "She's a beauty that's fer sure," he began, thinking to himself as he fought the urge to caress her cheek. With his luck with the girl, she'd probably wake up and catch him at it. Then fearful she'd wake up and see him spying on her, he decided he'd better try shaking her again.

"Kate, come on now! Get yerself inside! You'll catch yer death!"

"Keep botherin' me, Cinnie, and you'll catch yer death, too!" she called out again with another slap of her hand.

"Ah, Lord! The poor lass! I can't wake her up with her forgettin' her loss." Then looking down at his missing limb, he cursed himself for not having two good legs. "Damn nuisance, this!" he complained, slapping his thigh. "Takes me twice as much energy as a whole man!" he muttered to himself before wobbling off to the loft. The cat trailed behind him.

After lighting the lamp just inside the forge, he hopped his way up the ladder, waded through the room like a blind man, lit the lamp next to his bed, and grabbed up his leg. In a rush to attach it, he plopped down upon his bed nearly sitting on the cat, making both of them jump.

"What does she think she's doin' sleepin' on the porch?" he asked the cat when the answer came to him, making him pause, sigh deeply, and put his leg on the bed beside him so he could roll up his pant leg.

"She's makin' sure I made it home! That's it, isn't it cat?" With a meow as his answer, Nantze felt like he'd been kicked in the chest. "Ah! Why'd she want ta go and do that fer?" he asked the cat, and as before, the tom offered his opinion with the same simple reply. "Palfrey's right! She needs someone to take care of." Then doing a little digging into his own empty life, Nantze realized Palfrey was right about him, too. He needed mates. People to help him take his mind off his pain and his own worries.

"But a wife? Now that's a lot ta ask of a healthy man!" he huffed, picking up his leg to attach it.

"A wife is—well—a commitment! A man can't just go pop off 'will ya marry me,' ta some girl without knowing he can take care of her. I can hardly pull myself up a ladder!"

Then thinking of the girl still asleep on the porch, he tightened the buckle around his leg with more force than was needed. "My wife?" he said again, stood, and rubbed the stubble on his jaw. "That just canna be. I can hardly take care of myself!"

Within a few minutes, Nantze made his way back up the porch steps and shook Kate again. This time when she didn't move, he walked over and slipped open the front door, went back to her chair, grabbed her up in his arms, and carried her in. It was a strange awkward walk as he hobbled from his left to his right like a boat bobbing up and down between ripples.

Once inside, he carried her over to the chair by the fire. Intending to place her down with graceful ease, Nantze was quite shocked when the dog got caught up in his fake leg and tripped him up. Falling forward with the girl still in his arms, he landed with a thud face first into the high wing-back chair with Kate still in his arms. Grateful he hadn't crushed her, he righted his stance with his arms still wrapped around her.

In the dim light from the embers, which were still glowing in the grate, Nantze could see that she'd taken down her hair and put it in one long, thick braid. The lines of her face, too, were relaxed, and she smelled of lavender water. "Aye," he exhaled in a tender whisper. "Ya shouldn't have waited up fer me!" he reprimanded softly. "Ya've had as hard a day as I have."

Then overcome by his own emotions, he added in a raspy whisper, "Ya are the most beautiful little sprite, and I canna imagine the damn plaguey pain I'll endure when I leave here!" Thankfully for Nantze, she slept through both his confession and his trying to untangle his arms from around her. Hoping to make her comfortable, he bent down and placed the footstool at her feet, caressed her cheek, and smiled down at her for a long moment before pulling the blanket up around her chin, patting the dog's head, and sneaking out of the house as quietly as a man with one leg on crutches could ever hope to attain.

Moments after the door clicked shut and with Nantze's confused gait still heard wobbling down the porch steps, Kate exhaled a pent up breath and flicked away at the stream of tears running down her cheeks. Burying her face in her blanket, reciting the words he'd said, "Ya are the most beautiful little sprite," and cradling the small spark of hope to her heart, the corners of her lips turned upward and the ache in her chest lightened considerably.

∞∞∞∞

Chapter Six

That night, being physically exhausted, Nantze had just enough energy to kick the cat off the bed two times before he was sound asleep. However, sometime in the gloom of the wee morning hours before the sun broke across the horizon, the fool tom made the mistake of curling up by his chest, so when a cold nose pressed against his cheek and before the cat had time to retreat, it was flung violently through the air. Even before it landed on the floor with a thick thud, Nantze was dozing back to sleep with a satisfying smile pressed against his lips.

Later that morning shortly after the two had begun their work with Kate at the bellows and Nantze hammering the kinks out of one rod after another, he made a few of the rectangle frames needed for the fence. As he examined one to see how well it was joined, Kate seemed to slump at her post. "Watch that fire, lass," Nantze told her when the embers seemed more gray than red.

Within a moment the girl pumped air back into the coals. "I feel like these bellows," she began almost too quietly for him to hear. Realizing she needed to talk, he put down his tools and listened. "Like there is some unknown force pushin' air in and out of my lungs."

Moving from his work station to where she stood, he saw her emotions eating her countenance. "What is it Kate?"

"I don't think I can take this hurt!"

"Yer stronger than ya think!"

Shaking her head in disbelief, she added, "I canna stop seein' their bodies and hearin' the horse gasp and spit." Nantze tried to smile reassuringly into her upturned face. As he did so, she closed the eight-inch gap between them and rested the top of her forehead in the center of his chest. "I heard ya, last night afore ya left," she whispered. Heaving a small sigh, the torrent of pent up tears rushed from her eyes in a noiseless gush.

Standing motionless for some few minutes before cradling the nape of her neck with one hand and caressing her back with the other, Nantze cooed, "That's it. Just let it go! Let it go!" His mind, however, was rushing back to the night before and trying to remember what he'd said out loud.

The bottom line, however, was that she trusted him; therefore, he wanted to move slowly and allow her time to adjust to her new life. Perhaps she associated the loss of his limb to her own personal loss like Palfrey suggested or thought that he of all people would understand. He did, of course, but he also knew God had helped him. Now it seemed obvious, as he stood there like a bulwark for over a quarter of an hour, that God expected him to help her in return.

After some time, Nantze fished out his handkerchief and pushed it into her hand. Thankful for the proffered gift, she used it to sop up her sorrow. Untying her apron, he slipped it off over her head, led her to the pump, filled a cup, and made her drink it. Next he pulled down a towel from a nearby peg, wet it, and dabbed the cool rag on her face and the back of her neck. "You'll get stronger every day! I promise!"

Being fully spent, Kate barely nodded her acceptance of the fact as he led her to her porch chair. Behind the pair trotted the dog and following him came the cat.

Before he gave the action a proper amount of thought, Nantze reached out a tarnished hand, brushed away her hair, and gently caressed her cheek again before going back to the forge. Watching him go with the cat trailing behind him, a small smile turned the lady's lips upward. He was a good man and filled with understanding, so although she had been determined to keep him at arm's length, she found instead he helped fill the gap.

Over the next few days, the hefty mouser learned his boundaries. He knew not to jump upon the bed until the man's breathing leveled out and even then he knew not get within reach of his good leg or working arms. Nantze, too, learned his boundaries with the woman. She was certainly an interesting little thing with all her petals and thorns. Her beauty and harsh words.

Palfrey, on the other hand, had little trouble asking how Nantze was getting on when he came to pick him up that evening. "Well now, how's our lil' plan comin' 'long? 'Have ya given the lass a wee bit of a kiss yet?" the old man asked, his twin eyebrows arched mischievously as he poked his elbow in Nantze's ribs on the way to the Sow that night.

"I've not nor shall I, ya ol' duffer!" Nantze barked back. "Ya know as well as I do I'd more likely be mauled."

"Mauled, indeed, not Miracle Nantze!" he began with a low chuckle and a slap on his boney knee. "Ya give the lass courage!"

"Hmmph!" Nantze balked. However, the more he thought about some of the things that had happened so far, he had to acknowledge that Palfrey might be right. Thinking of how she allowed him to hold her hand, how she rested her head on his chest, and the way she'd been helping him in the forge every morning, Nantze was surprised to realize she'd been, for the most part, amazingly open with him. "Either that or she just needs someone ta laugh at!" he added under his breath, talking to himself.

"What's that?" Palfrey asked.

Trying to decide how much of this morning's antics he should share with the spry old man, Nantze finally said, "Oh, as I said the other night, that cat's taken it into its head we're friends or at least my bum leg is his new, favorite scratchin' post. I tell ya, Palfrey, I canna stop in one place too long or that fool tom thinks I'm offerin' him an invitation. I've near trip over him, stepped on his tail, and just about dropped my hammer on him!" Nantze told his friend with a shake of his head. "And that ol' hound ain't no better!"

"Ya don't say?" Palfrey offered, hoping Nantze would expound, which he did.

"Follows the girl, of course, as he should, but the fool thing's gettin' deaf and takes up residence right under the table where the anvil sits."

"Yeah, go on!" Palfrey nudged, his twin brows arched upward in anticipation.

"Soon as I starts poundin' away at somethin', that fool dog shoots up out from under the table straight into my metal leg. Well, up go my arms, hammer in one hand, molten-hot, iron rod in the other, and all the while I'm steppin' backwards behind myself tryin' ta get a steady grip on my footwork. Wouldn't ya know it, that's the prime time that tom decides ta take off after a wee beastie somewhere on the other side of the forge and runs between my feet just as I'm gettin' myself steady. Next thin' I know, I'm hoppin' up and down like a fool tryin' ta get outta the way! Only when I hops up and down, it looks more like I'm one of those wooden puppets on a stick with all my limbs movin' in quick, jerky movements. Up goes the hammer and hot iron. Up goes my good leg with a hop and when it hits the ground, up goes my bad one. Aye, then down they all go again. I looked like I was leadin' an iron worker's parade!"

Imagining all of Nantze's comical movements, Palfrey let out a hoot, sending his eyebrows skyward again.

"Aye, that's exactly what Kate did! I swear the girl laughed over a minute straight!"

"I don't think I could blame her fer that!" Palfrey offered, slapping his own knee in delight.

"Nor could I. It's how she looked when she laughed that drove a stake through my heart, I tell ya!"

"What'd ya mean?" Palfrey asked, suddenly concerned. "Did her eyes not look merry, and her face flush a colorful crimson, like it aught?"

"Aye, she never looked more beautiful, and I never felt more lame in my life! Palfrey, that girl ain't gonna want no broken down man like me! I couldn't even carry her in the cottage the other night without bunglin' the job. Nearly broke my nose fallin' into the chair with the girl in my arms!"

"Carried her in, eh?"

"Aye," he began, waving the man away. "She fell asleep on the porch, and I couldn't wake her ta go inside. Goin' back to the loft, I puts on my leg, limps my way back to the porch, picks her up, and hobbles her ta that great chair by the fire she's always in. Wouldn't ya know it, my bum leg caught on the dog and landed me in the chair face first with the girl still in my arms."

His eyebrows dancing like waves across his forehead, Palfrey's clear blue eyes sparkled. "I knewed it! Saw it the moment we met."

Rolling his eyes, Nantze tried changing the subject. "Are any of the men looking at anyone else fer the position? Mayhap there's a better man fer the job!"

"No, nor will we!" Palfrey told him, pulling up his horse to a stop in front of the Yellow Sow. "I, fer one, have already found the man what's needed fer this here scenario, so there's no need me wastin' my time lookin' at anyone else! Ye just finish out yer week and leave me ta figure out how ta handle the girl!"

Shaking his head and wobbling down from the seat, Nantze sighed. "I'm not as worried about her as I am me. Girl's got my gut in knots!" Nantze spouted off and received nothing more than a toothless grin from his friend. Seeing that all further talk on the subject was useless, Nantze said no more about it. It wouldn't do any good if he did. Palfrey, the old codger, was as stubborn as he was superstitious.

However as talk at the Sow moved to how quickly time was going by and how much work still needed to be finished, the black-tipped caterpillars on Palfrey's brow descended into a low brooding line. He had to acknowledge that there was no getting away from the fact that Nantze's week was coming to a swift end, and Kate hadn't said anything about his staying or starting any other projects. Nantze had made great progress on the fence, of course, and was expected to be ready to plant the solid, wrought-iron posts in their places on the day after next. Once that was done, so was his week.

On the following evening after filling his belly with Kincaid's hearty stew and having had the subject of setting the fencing breeched, Nantze reminded the men of his need for a cart and horse, and it was decided that both Palfrey and Kincaid would help haul the fence portions, and anyone else who wanted to see the progress could swing round when they had time.

So bright and early, almost before Nantze was able to finish his weak tea and measly grub, Palfrey was in the yard rattling off a premonition he'd had about Saint Peter himself peering down out of heaven to survey the work.

"What's that yer sayin'?" Nantze asked as the old man spryly jumped down from the seat of his horse drawn cart.

"I saw a vision!"

Shaking his head, Nantze simply decided to wait.

"In the wee hours right afore a body fully wakes, I heard my name. 'Palfrey,' I hears, and I says, 'Yes, Lord?' Next I sees us puttin' in these fence sections around the Cathedral, and a beam, bright as the Christmas star, leaps down out of heaven and shines all 'round us!"

"Well then, we best not keep yer vision waitin', eh?" Nantze offered as the two began loading fence sections onto Palfrey's cart. "Help me grab up this one here, will ya?" Nantze asked then moved to the center to heft it to the cart.

Palfrey learned quickly that his job wasn't to help carry. It was to balance. Every time Nantze took a step on his metal leg, the right side of the load drooped toward the ground. It was Palfrey's job to shove the load level again. This strange exercise being repeated with each new section of fencing became as organized as any ballet. Bad leg, push. Good leg, hold. Bad leg, push. Good leg, hold.

"Well now, if the two of ya don't make a picture!" Kincaid laughed as he pulled his team to stop.

"We're a well-oiled machine!" Palfrey spit out, getting into the rhythm of Nantze's lopsided method.

"I can quite easily see that!" Kincaid shot back with a smile. Within moments, he gathered up sections of fencing and put them in the back of his cart. Between the three of them, they had the job done in little time.

They were just ready to leave the yard when Kate came bounding out of the house in a black dress. "Wait, I'm comin' with ya!" Her hair was braided in, what seemed to Nantze, a complete semi-circle behind her head, which ran from ear to ear. The style seemed to soften all her hard edges, and tiny tendrils curled around the base of her neck and around her ears, giving her an inviting sort of look that, according to Nantze, was probably not accurate.

Palfrey, seeing an opportunity to throw the two together, handed the reins at Nantze, hopped down, helped Katie onto the seat, and carried himself over to Kincaid's rig before pulling himself upon on the seat next to him.

"We'll lead the way!" Palfrey hollered over his shoulder, and Nantze could do nothing more than follow along behind.

Taking his life into his own hands, Nantze decided to be brave. "Right nice day!" he began as he looked down at the girl at his side.

"Aye it is. I imagine with the aid of all these men, ya should get things set quickly!"

"With so many hands, I suppose we will. The curate has assured me all the holes have been dug." Looking over at the girl, he smiled down reassuringly at her. She was going on an outing, which, except for going to the Sow when he'd come, she'd not done since her father had died.

"Palfrey and ya seem ta be becomin' good mates!" Katie offered dryly when the old man turned around to observe Nantze's progress.

"Does the ol' codger stick his nose in everybody's pie or just ours?"

"Do we have pie?"

"Did I say ours? I meant mine."

"What's he been doin'?"

"Never mind! I should keep quiet, I'm sure."

"Ya should say what yer thinkin'!" she told him harshly. "I'm not a child!"

Taking a few moments to weigh out the value in telling her what he really thought about her and about working the forge, he nodded his head and unhinged his jaw again. Looking down at her, his eyes soften considerably. "I find I like the boss, but...!"

"Now ya wait just a minute, Nantze!" Katie spat out. "Palfrey isn't the boss! I bloody well am!"

"I know Kate, nor were I talkin' about Palfrey!" he returned patiently.

"Oh," she replied, halting her anger and transforming it into understanding. "Ya do?"

"I do, but..." he tried to continue.

"Ya don't find me all needles and thorns, then?" she interrupted again.

Laughter filled his eyes, making them sparkled as the corner of his lip curled upward, transforming his face. "No, Kate. I don't, but..."

Then a new idea jumped into her mind and out her mouth. "Don't think if I ask ya ta stay that I'll marry ya!" Pointing a finger in his direction, she accented each of her words with a stabbing motion. "Because I won't!"

Not waiting for her to come up with something else, Nantze spoke in slow even tones charged with that power that never failed to surprised her. "I've not asked ya ta marry me, Kate," he began but was interrupted again. This time more contritely.

"Oh, right." Whispering, she looked down at her hands and alternately crunched them into small fists on her lap then opened them again.

Seeing her pinch down on her lips to keep herself from saying something as equally embarrassing and not wanting the girl to have any misconceptions about him staying if he did choose to stay, he continued, "Nor have I asked ya ta keep me like I'm some stray ya've picked up."

"I've not treated ya like some..." Seeing his look, she pinched her lips shut again.

"Nor, since I have yer attention, FINALLY, do I like the way ya act like yer doin' me some grand favor either! Like yer takin' me in. I've already got a job, Kate, and I make a fine livin' fer a single man with almost no expenses of my own. I take my wage and store it up, so that when this bum leg goes completely lame, I'll have a roof over my head. More than that, woman, I have pride. So I'd appreciate it greatly if ya'd stop actin' like I'm lookin' fer a handout from ya! I'm damn good at my work, and if ya'd like ta know, I'm good at inventin', solvin' problems, and engineerin'. Even the railroad's asked me ta take up a job, but I told 'em I was comin' here first ta see about this opportunity."

The morning glow bounced off her dark hair, creating a halo that was impossible for Nantze to ignore. She was a beautiful girl, it was true, but angelic she was not. It was time she stopped thinking so much of her own sorrow and looked at the facts.

"As I said, like ya, but I've got pride. And I've no intentions of cozyin' up ta ya ta get yer forge! Beyond that I don't want a wife. A man like me ought not ta marry. It'd be selfish of me." Having said his peace, the two followed Kincaid's cart in silence.

"A man like what?" she whispered a little later.

"A broken one, Kate! Can ya imagine what would happen if I got hurt or what this ol' leg will be like when I get old?" When she didn't answer, he went on. "If'n ya can't, I can! I'll be a damn rickety sight, ta be sure, and by that time, I'd be a burden to ya. That makes the idea of marriage, ta me, repellent."

Not knowing what to say, Katie clenched her hands in her lap. Seeing how bound up she was, he threw his head back in submission, reached over, and placed his own hand on top of hers. When she looked up at him, he smiled reassuringly and said, "Mayhap, though, we might work very well one with another. Ya need a smithy, and I like the idea of stayin'." After this small speech the two became silent. Each lost in their own thoughts of weighing out the pros and cons of her offering the position and him taking it.

Before long, Palfrey, sitting next to Kincaid on the cart in front of them, turned around and tried to catch Nantze's eye. The old codger attempted to be nonchalant as he turned around on the bench, shot a meaningful glance at Nantze, and bobbed his head toward Kate, indicating that Nantze should be wooing the girl sitting next to him.

When his first attempts didn't work, Palfrey became more animated in his efforts, raised his bushy eyebrows in perfect arches, and jerked his head back and forth in erratic movements, motioning toward the girl. His tactics became so ridiculous and obvious that Nantze had a hard time holding back a grin. "Is Palfrey tryin' ta tell ya somethin'?" Kate finally asked.

"I can only wonder!"

"What is it Palfrey?" she finally called out. Shocked that she noticed him, his eyebrows popped up in unison, and he jumped in surprise. His mouth, too, drew up into a perfect little o, and he spun back around in his seat, making Nantze hoot with laughter. The sound of which cascaded around Kate, and she giggled, which turned into a hearty laugh and was followed by a very clear snort.

Covering her mouth with one dainty gloved hand, she laughed again, releasing her angst like a landslide until a sweet lopsided smile was visible upon her face, transforming her countenance and melting her reserve—a little. "I'm sorry."

Smiling, Nantze nodded at her. It was time to let his words simmer in her mind, so the two rode on in silence despite Palfrey's varied attempts at getting them to pay attention to each other.

The setting of the fence itself was difficult for a one-leg man. Luckily for Nantze, Kincaid organized a number of men to carry the sections and place them in the holes. Along with those who wished to be helpful, came many more men whose only desire was to watch or give advice.

The curate was especially philosophical, having spent days in determining the best way Nantze should do the work he was hired to do. However, Providence thankfully intervened on his behalf, and Kincaid was at hand to sidetrack the curate's constant good intentions with boisterous reminders of Nantze's ability as a craftsman.

Once each of the sections were properly installed, those who had come to inspect the work declared it a success. Nantze, however, weary, worn, and weak, hobbled himself to Palfrey's cart, yanked up his pants, and removed his leg. While those there to see the finished project went to point out the quality of the work to Kate and give their opinion about Nantze staying on as smithy.

"Well now, Kate? Ya gonna ask the man ta stay, I suppose. Can't see that we'd find anyone half so adept as this man here is," Kincaid offered as they all stood back and admired the finished product. "Right nice bloke, too, says I."

Kate, however, didn't offer a reply. Nor did she comment when Pippen the Sweep asked if Nantze would be around to twist his broom handles.

"Well fer a woman whose words fall on the ear like a lead pipe, yer exceptionally quiet!" Kincaid called out in his boisterous way when she didn't answer any of the questions posed to her.

"Aye, lassie," Palfrey added, "What says ye?"

"I haven't made up my mind yet."

"Good Lord and Heaven above lass! Ya've had an entire week!" Kincaid belted out as he pointed at the expertly constructed gate surrounding the cathedral, which as Palfrey had envisioned, was bathed in a shaft of light.

Then one of the onlookers, a Mr. Coggins, aided the conversation by saying, "Leave it ta a woman not ta know her own mind." This, of course, sparked no few snide remarks and sideways glances. In fact, a few of the men were brave enough to offer a smirk and a muffled laugh.

Seeing how the gentlemen were becoming less like what their name suggested they were the longer they spoke, Nantze called out, "Kate, my leg's a might sore. Jump up here and lead the way back ta the forge will ya?"

Seeing her chance to leave in a quiet, demure manner, Kate picked up her skirt and, in her defense, considered leaving without a smarting retort, but found she didn't have the stomach for it.

Therefore, turning on Coggins, she called out, "And what do ya know about a woman's mind, Coggins, seein' as ya've never de-lighted a woman's heart nor gotten one ta so much as dance with ya." This caused the man's eyes to ogle in surprise, and while all of the men were watching his reaction, Kate loaded her lead shot for another round.

"And another thing!" This time she pointed at a number of the men to let them know that these words were aimed at them. "The forge belongs ta me! If'n I choose ta shut it down, it's my own busi-ness, and I won't be havin' the likes of ya bullyin' me inta doin' somethin' I am not ready ta do!"

With each of the men sufficiently stupefied and their shocked unbelief clearly displayed across their faces like goods in a shop window, she turned her back upon them to go, but as Nantze watched the drama unfold like a one act play, he saw a new idea move across Kate's features, and shook his head.

In a moment, she reeled back around, making the men all take one step's retreat. This time when she spoke, she was more spe-cific. "And scoff at me again, Milton Mayer, and you'll be getting yer smith work done elsewhere! That goes fer you, too, Jamison Newbry! As if'n I don't have eyes. You might not of let the words go, but they were written on yer face!"

Having had their names called out, both men jumped like naughty school boys who hadn't known the teacher was behind them until they were struck on the back of their necks with a fag-got of reeds.

Having gained considerable steam, Kate added, "You fools seem ta think I'm beholdin' ta ya fer forcin' me ta hire a man when I canna even listen ta the pin' of the hammer without seein'... without bein' reminded..."

Taking her sorrow as an opportunity to escort her to the wagon, Palfrey took Kate by the arm and cooed, "Aye, lass! We're doin' our best by ya, and ya knows that well enough!" As Palfrey led her toward the wagon, the men stepped aside to let her pass. Some of them even offered up their apologies.

"Dinna mean ta upset ya, lass."

"We only want what's best fer ya, Kate!"

"Aye, I'm sorry Kate!" Pippen the Sweep began in his shy, hawish way, "I shouldn't have pressed ya."

Stopping in front of him as she walked past, Kate reached out her hand and patted his. "None of that was fer ya, Ellis Pippen!" she told him, using his familiar name. "You've not a meddlin' bone in ya, ta be sure!"

Smiling under her uncharacteristically kind words, the man beamed. Then turning to Palfrey, who was still leading her to the wagon, she added, "I know yer doin' yer best fer me, ya 'ol duffer, but some of these fools here have naught ta say about it, and I won't have 'em treatin' me in this ungentlemanly manner!"

"Just so, lass!" Handing her up into the rig, Palfrey smiled. "Off with ya. It's too late fer him ta leave today. There's time enough fer the two of ya ta come ta an agreement." Slapping his horse's flank to get the old hag moving, Palfrey stepped aside.

Nantze, needing to rub down his swollen stump, retrieved a salve from his trousers' pocket and handed Katie the ribbons.

The men, still somewhat shell-shocked, watched the cart disappear over a small swell and bend in the landscape before daring to speak. "Aye, that daff, lil' fire-sprite doesn't know what's best fer her!" Kincaid finally ventured as all of the men began to disperse, each man going to his own rig.

"We needs that man ta stay!" Pippen the Sweep added and many of the men from their small hamlet, those who frequented the Yellow Sow, nodded their agreement as they walked together toward where they'd left their horses.

"Providence deemed this job a priority, surely. The girl can do as she wishes as far as I am concerned," the curate told Kincaid with a surly nod.

"And that from a man o' God!" Palfrey bellowed, his twin caterpillars furrowing into an offended line.

"Blast ya, ya arrogant fool! Don't ya see that if that man leaves here, we'll be burying the lass next ta her mother!" Kincaid spat back as Palfrey nodded his agreement.

"Well now, there's no cause to rattle me so. I don't want the girl to pine away, I'm sure!" the curate answered back with less condescending tones.

"We have ta come up with somethin'! The girl's about ta blow away in a breeze as she is." Pippen the Tailor piped in, causing his brother to noticeably quiver at the thought.

"I'm workin' on that end of the puzzle. I ain't quite hit on the plan, but I promise ya, she'll keep the man." Palfrey's caterpillar brows rose hopefully, and he added, "Ye just waits! I'll hit on an idea yet!"

"Ya've less than a day ta do it!" Kincaid reminded him as their small group reached their rigs and mounts.

"Aye, but I tell ya the truth, Nantze is the miracle we've been prayin' fer!"

"I hope so. I like Kate!" Pippen the Sweep moped.

As the men got to where their mounts were tied, Pippin the Tailor scratched his head and said, "Ellis, is it?" as he looked at his brother. "I thought that were my name." And even Palfrey gave a small hoot of laughter.

∞ ∞ ∞

"Ya did a fine job," Kate whispered as she watched Nantze rub down his stump, concern edged like ruts around her large doe eyes. "Most likely over did it, I'd say."

Her eyes were kindly at the moment. "All pedals and perfume," thought Nantze as he looked at her before explaining, "Today was my last, and I'm a man of my word."

Not knowing what else to say and because she had so many thoughts rolling around in her mind, Kate kept her tongue tied between her teeth except for an occasional command to the horse. Part of her wanted to tell Nantze to go to the devil, and that she'd just as soon never hear the ping of a hammer again.

She'd even thought out verbatim what she would say to get him to leave. She could easily imagine, too, how he'd nod his head with kind understanding, thank her for considering him, and hobble away to gather his few effects. However every time she thought of him leaving, she could see her cat loyally trotting off behind him. In fact, no matter how she came at the dilemma, the outcome ran a similar course and ended with her in deep emotional pain.

Hurting considerably more than he could handle at the moment, Nantze closed his eyes and tried to rest; however, when he heard Kate draw a quick intake of breath, he opened his eyes to see that they were nearing the bend in the road where the Cinnies had died. Without thought, he put his arm around her shoulders, pulled her small frame across the wooden bench, and pressed her head to rest against his arm.

"Close yer eyes, Kate," There was no need for him to say so. She couldn't see through the unshed tears anyway. Pulling his handkerchief from his pocket, he handed it to her and took the reins. Clucking to the mare, the two rode the rest of the way home with Nantze's strong arm clutching the girl to his side while he intermediately whispered kind retorts and kissed the top of her feather-soft head.

He'd forgotten to bring his crutches that morning but so loathed the idea of asking Katie to fetch them for him that he began to attach the leg to his raw, red stump. Getting gingerly down, he waited for Kate to scoot to his side of the bench seat, so that he might help her, but as independent as ever, she looked at his outstretched arm and the pained look in his eyes and clambered down from her side. "Go take care of yer leg. I'm fine."

Smiling at her and making her heart swell when he did so, Nantze pulled his worn work bag full of tools out of the boot of the cart and struggled to carry them back to the forge. In fact, he was headed in that direction when Palfrey and Kincaid came lumbering up the cart road and called out their greetings.

Pulling his rig to a stop to let Palfrey collect his rig, Kincaid called out, "Shall we see ya at the Sow later?"

"Aye, and I'll be hungry when I get there!" Nantze told him, rubbing his empty stomach as he said so.

"I'll be sure ta have a feast prepared," Kincaid answered back.

Not wanting to stay overly long, Palfrey walked into the forge to take his leave.

"I'll come round after a bit. Get yerself off that leg!"

"That I'll do and in a hurry!" Nantze proclaimed and began pulling himself up the ladder.

As Palfrey made his way home in his pony cart, the widow Crone, aided by a spindly walking stick and the arm of her decrypted sister, pulled Palfrey up short by raising her cane into the air. When he looked at them, the two women leveled him with a disturbing stare, and Crone barked out in a thick, raspy voice, "Who's next in line ta inherit the smithy?"

"When Kate goes the way of the rest of her brood?" her sister, Harpy, added in the same strange voice.

"By the looks of her, it'll not be too long afore she gives up the ghost!" Crone continued, her pallid skin looking like it was melting down her face as she spoke.

Being utterly offended at the old hags' speech, Palfrey's twin caterpillar brows descended into a menacing line, and he pulled his horse to swift stop. "Don't go around heapin' people's plates with yer damn dark sundries! You'll invite Death ta come 'round sure as there's a sunrise."

"Anyone with eyes can see Kate's pinnin' away," Crone began with a jeer.

"And ye?" her sister hissed as she pointed a spindly finger at him.

"Pretendin' ta help the girl by hirin' a lame man ta do the work of the Cinnies!" old lady Crone finished for her sister.

"Ya damn fool!" said Harpy.

"Yer only prolongin' her demise!" finished her sister.

"Off with ya! Witches!" he yelled. "My Kate'll come 'round!"

Scoffing at his optimism, Crone spat back, "She'll melt away!"

"Unless ya can figure a way ta get her ta put some meat in her belly!" her crooked little hag of a sister spat then both nodded their heads at Palfrey to verify that they had said their peace and done their duty by the girl, God, and all that was holy.

Palfrey, however, was so disturbed by the witches' conversation that his mind began to spin through all of the various schemes he'd dreamed up this past week to ensure that Nantze wormed his way into the girl's affections. All of his ideas, however, had hit upon a way to get Kate to keep him not for him to save her.

Replaying what the old woman said, "She will unless ya can figure out a way to get her to put some meat in her belly," Palfrey hit upon the simplest and most obvious conclusion, making him agog that he shouldn't have thought of it before now, and although Palfrey did not like the way the hags phrased their prophecy, they did hit upon the missing link. Therefore, placing all of his thoughts in the same bowl and whisking them around for the few minutes it took him to make his way back home, Palfrey ruminated on an idea, that if played out properly, would solve the trifold problem created by the loss of Cin and son.

∞ ∞ ∞

Chapter Seven

"**W**hat now, ya ol' duffer! Ya look like ya've seen another ghost!" Ivy cooed when he entered their small thatched cottage looking pale and sickly.

"Those plaguey sisters Grimm! They were poppin' off how my girl's goin' the way of her brood. Said she'd die if'n we couldn't get her ta eat somethin'."

"Tis true, surely. She's naught but a wisp."

"Those ghouls and their dark sundries! It was probably them what done it in the first place!" Palfrey seethed, his furry caterpillar brows descending into a fierce line.

"Done what?" Ivy asked, as she cut a healthy slice of bread and buttered it. Handing it to her husband, she listened thoughtfully.

Taking a large bite and sucking down a swallow of tea, he explained, "Conjured up that caped reaper I saw afore the Cinnies died."

"Oh, if'n ya don't set a store of reliance on such foolish notions!" Taking the knife, chunking off a large wedge of cheese, and placing it on the end of a skewer to toast, she rolled her eyes.

"I tell ya, that were no vision, woman. It were as real as ye." When she looked crossways at him, he added, "and as terrifying." Thinking his joke was particularly fitting, he grinned, exposing his missing teeth.

Slapping him with a rag she used to open the lid on the cast iron pot, Ivy shook her head. "Ya ol' duffer."

Watching his wife piddle about the place preparing his meal, he realized it might be the missing link. "Aye, I might get the girl ta respond yet!"

"Did she agree ta hire him, then?" Ivy asked, placing the cheese in front of her husband before topping of his tea and ladling up a hearty portion of stew from the pot hanging in the hearth.

"No, the little sprite!" he began, truly vexed with the girl.

"She's never been one ta be told what she should do, that's fer certain."

Thinking of what had happened at the cathedral earlier, he snorted. "Aye and ya should have seen her Ivy, given some of those men an earful. We got the fence up alright and tight. Looks like a masterpiece! Well, no sooner had the job got done then they started railin' her about hirin' the man in earnest." As Palfrey spoke, his twin caterpillar danced around his brow—sometimes going up as high as the middle of his forehead—other times descending so low as to make his eyes disappear altogether.

"Well, ya ol' codger, what'd she say that's got ya so ready to bound across the room?" she asked, filling her own bowl.

"When one or another of the men asked if she was gonna offer him the job, she said she'd not yet made up her mind. That's when that slick fool, Coggins, goes and pops off that it was just like a woman not ta know her own mind."

"Ha and what does an old fish like him know about a woman's mind, I wonder?"

"If'n that isn't exactly what Kate wanted ta know!" he added, slapping his hands together. "Mayer, bein' one what's never kept his lips closed, let loose a laugh, so she turned on him too! Said, 'Scoff at me again Melton Mayer and you'll be takin' yer smith work elsewhere!"

"Aye that lass can spit lead balls when she's a mind ta." Bowing her head and giving thanks, the two paused a moment before spooning dinner into their mouths.

"And she wasn't done yet," he clamored excitedly. "Told all

those fancy men what had come ta watch better men than 'em do the work that she'd not allow 'em ta bully her into a decision that was none of their business. Then she said they was ungentle-manly!"

"That ought ta set them down a few rungs!"

"What I says is, that's just the kind o' fight the girl needs ta get her blood up! Brings out the spirit in her!"

"Mayhap she'll scare that man Nantze away with such feisty conduct. I hears he's a right handsome bloke."

"Not as well as me, but not one ta sour the cream either, says me."

"Ya ol' duffer!" Ivy cooed and squeezed his hand from across the table. "Thinkin' yerself a charmer, eh?"

"Charmed you, didn't I?"

"Yes, but my eyes are bad," she volleyed.

"Wound me, will ya?" This statement was churlish enough not only to make his twin caterpillars go on the offensive but his scruffy gray sideburns also rose in mock offence.

"Remind ya of yer place, more like!" his wife tossed back, and the two shared a chuckle.

Still ruminating over the best way to get Kate to take care of herself, Palfrey set out to get Nantze shortly after he'd finished his meal. Hopefully he'd not over stressed his leg; however, even as he thought it, he contradicted it. "Mayhap the man is too independ-ent!" he cried out with some energy as he clicked at his horse and pulled him out on the cart road.

Adding this idea to the others, Palfrey mulled it over, and was still considering possible scenarios and speeches he might or-chestrate to play upon Kate's natural sympathies, which he knew were few. "Still," he thought to himself, "there is a heart o' gold hidden under all those sharp angles and points," he whispered to himself as he pulled up into Kate's yard.

Being more famished than normal, Nantze was waiting and hobbled over quickly before Palfrey had even told his old nag to whoa. "What be eatin' at ya, Nantze? Ya in a hurry ta leave?"

"It's not what's been eatin' at me, but what I've not been eatin'.

I'm famished!"

"Why that's it!" Palfrey chimed, putting all his thoughts in order.

"What is?" Nantze asked without caring as he nodded his head for Palfrey to make haste. "I can't survive another day such as this one was with little more than bread and cheese for a noon meal, that's what. Mayhap it's best I move on," he concluded. "I'm a man what's gotta eat."

With his own thoughts raging through his head and a toothless grin exposing the gaps in his dentistry, Palfrey clucked the horse in to a swift canter, and when he saw Nantze's harried, lopsided walk going into the Sow, he praised it as a blessing that his new friend was both starving and in pain. "Yes, that will do just fine!" the old codger cooed.

Seeing the pair come in, Kincaid looked up. "I'll have yer food ready, directly!" He loaded up Nantze's nightly tray, and set it before him as soon as it was ready.

"Well?" Kincaid asked Palfrey as the spry little man sat at the bar with a smile on his lips.

"Not yet," he clucked.

Irritated, Kincaid called out, "She's not made ya an offer?"

Ignoring the question while he bowed his head and gave thanks, Nantze didn't answer until he'd shoveled in and swallowed two heaping mouthfuls and a bite of bread and cheese. Seeing the way he fell on the food, Kincaid cast a questioning look at Palfrey.

"Boy's not eatin' enough," he offered with a smile.

"Aye, makes me appreciate my other job in Lancaster. I ate like a king!"

"Well, what about the lass?" Kincaid asked again as all of the men in the Sow quieted down to hear the answer.

"Looks like she'd rather earn her funds another way."

"Surely, her good sense," Pippen the Sweep began.

"Would override her pain," his brother finished.

"That's just what I think!" Pippen the Sweep nodded to the assembly.

When no one else spoke, Kincaid finally said in a huff, "So, you'll be off then?"

"Aye, I'll either go back ta Lancaster or take a job with the railroad."

"Railroad!" the Pippen brothers called out in unison.

"They offered me a job as I was boardin' the train ta come see about this work here," Nantze told them, drawing on his draught and refilling his spoon.

After this small speech and as Nantze was busy biting off a crust of bread with butter, the men threw knowing looks between one another. With little more to say on the subject and having filled his gullet to capacity, Nantze picked up his crutches, nodded to his friends, and promised he'd come around on the morrow to say goodbye before he headed back on the train.

Palfrey, however, seemed to be unaffected by the forlorn feelings of his friends, and it was remarked upon by some of the men after he left that he seemed happy to see Nantze go.

"Palfrey was in uncommonly good spirits," MacMurphy noticed and commented. "Seems rather odd, him takin' such a likin' ta Nantze."

"Aye, I thought as much myself."

"Almost seems..." Pippen the Sweep started.

"Like he's happy," his brother finished.

With a look of angry suspicion, Kincaid crossed his arms over his barrel chest. "If I know anythin' about that ol' codger, Palfrey, he's got somethin' up his sleeve," he offered, having known the spry, old goat since he was a lad.

"Aye, I like him!" Pippen the Sweep mumbled into his jar.

"Right! We don't wanna see the man leave!" his twin added as he pointed back and forth between himself and his brother.

"What I says is, Kate's become almost approachable!" added Jimmy MacMarker as he unconscientious rubbed the eye she'd blackened so many years ago. "Why she was downright gentle to Pippen the Sweep. And I ain't ever seen her do that afore!"

"Less like needles and thorns, I tell you, she's never been," Hardy, the postmaster continued. "There was a day she'd of given those men a set down they'd not likely soon forget."

"Now that's certain!" Kincaid added harshly. "Besides that I rather like the man myself and have a mind ta let that lil' fire-spitter know it!"

"The Londoner said he were a miracle man." MacMurphy reminded them.

"Mayhap he were right!"

"Aye, fer all of us, I hope he was!" Kincaid added, and all the men agreed.

Riding along in silence with his head nodding to one side on occasion, Nantze was anxious to get in between the sheets, and feeling exhausted like he was, he told Palfrey with a yawn, "I might not even kick the cat off the bed tonight."

"Well now, that is gracious of ya." Palfrey laughed before adding lightly, "I think I'll just go talk ta Kate a minute afore ya retire fer the night." Taking that to mean that he was to wait on his return, Nantze decided to make a few adjustments on his leg before setting out tomorrow.

∞ ∞ ∞

Chapter Eight

Palfrey, finding Kate sitting in the darkening gloom of her front parlor, brought up the subject of having Nantze stay long enough to get some of the other projects her par had been working on finished.

"Now there Kate, ya know as well as I do, ya need the man ta stay. We canna go lookin' all over again fer a man what's able ta do the job as proficiently as he's been able ta do. At least let him finish up all those small jobs the men are needin' done, and I hadn't mentioned it afore, but that iron monstrosity yer par was haulin' needs ta be fixed and returned."

"I don't think I'm ready ta be constantly hearin' the beat of the hammer in the forge," the girl whispered from her father's overstuffed chair, her dog lying at her feet.

"Ya have lil' choice. Ya canna support yerself if'n ya let the man go. He's a good man, works hard, keeps ta himself, and don't go about botherin' ya, does 'he?"

"Aye, e 'keeps ta himself."

"Ya have a problem with his skill, then?"

"No, Palfrey. I don't."

"Ya don't like him then, I suppose?"

"No, he's a fine man," she whispered.

"What is it then, lass? Ya know ya canna live without an income."

"It's too soon. I canna take hearin' him out there all hours bangin' away like Cinny and my par used ta do. Breaks my heart!"

"Well then," he paused and exhaled loudly, "I'll send him away." He then stood to go, and began walking out the front door. He slumped appropriately as he left. His eyes, however, held a merry twinkle. Even his twin caterpillar brows looked to be doing a swift Irish jig, making it apparent he wasn't done playing his cards no matter what Kate said.

Watching Palfrey, Kate's eyes filled with tears. The idea of having Nantze leave was suddenly more cumbersome than having him stay, and she cried out. "NO!"

Turning back to look at her after he'd had a moment to subdue his brows into a line, Palfrey asked, "What do ya want, lass? I canna help ya if'n ya don't know yer own mind."

"I don't want the man ta stay, but I canna let him go either." Then looking at Palfrey and terrified that he might tell Nantze what she said, she added, "And don't ya go flappin' yer jaws about it either, ya duffer!"

"Well, do I tell the man ya'd like him ta go or are ya plannin' ta offer him the job? 'I'm tellin' ya ta yer face, a man like him's got options. In fact, he could get a job anywheres he likes. What are ya prepared ta offer him ta get him ta stay?"

"What da ya mean?"

"The railroad wants ta hire him and promises ta pay him a king's wage fer his troubles."

"That were mentioned today."

"Aye, and his job in Lancaster puts meat on his plate thrice daily at no charge! So if'n ya want the man ta stay..." Palfrey offered but let the words drop like stones in the silence of her thoughts.

When the girl didn't reply. Palfrey answered the question he could see floating around in her mind.

"I'm not ginna tell ya what ta do lass! It's yer smithy, but I will say, I rather doubt you'll find a better man at his trade or a kinder one."

After a long pause, she answered. "Aye, ask him ta stay, but what do ya suppose I should offer him?"

"What says ya ta forty percent of the profits and his room in the loft?"

"Seems fair. What'd the railroad offer?"

"Don't rightly know. Dinna say."

"What if'n it's not enough?"

"Then ya offer him more, I 'spect."

"Who'll be the one ta tell him?"

"I'll do it if'n ya want."

"I do."

Then rattling off in his way Palfrey headed for the door and stopped. "The man's lookin' puny survivin' on whatever food he scrounges up of a day. Mayhap, he won't want ta stay. Let's face it girl, ya might need ta consider feedin' the man, or just like yer doin' ta yerself, he'll be worn ta a thread!"

When Kate didn't answer, he went on. "Should of seen the way he fell on Kincaid's stew tonight. Twas like he were starvin'," he told her with a shake of his head.

"I'm not ready ta feed the man and that's final."

"Suit yerself, but the man's got ta eat. And it might be he won't wanna stay under such circumstances!" Leaving the girl to do a little stewing of her own over what Nantze was used to getting for his wage and wanting to tell Nantze the good news, Palfrey took himself over to the forge where his new friend was just reattaching his leg.

"Thought ya was goin' ta bed?"

"Just makin' some adjustments fer my journey," he told him, stepping gingerly on his fake leg to test out his adjustments.

"Well now, mayhap ya won't need ta take that journey, Nantze. We men are all in agreement, so I put it afore the girl. She wants ta offer ya the job at forty percent of the profits, and ya get ta live in the loft. I bet she'll even throw in the cat if'n ya want!"

"Well now, the cat, that is generous isn't it?" Nantze answered, thinking over the idea. "Won't get that from the railroad will I?"

"There's a lot ya won't get from the railroad. They'll just pay ya yer wage and expect ya ta slave away ta whatever tune they fancy. Most likely have ya runnin' all over the jolly island. Beyond that, with Katie the more ya get done the greater yer wage. More importantly, ya get to choose when yer done fer the day, and that ya won't get anywhere else, I'd wager."

"Well with that and the cat, it seems like quite a bargain!" He smiled and exhaled. He'd not realized how much he'd grown attached to the girl.

"Don't discount the fact that you'll be workin' fer yerself, too! Be able to manage things as ya like. Not ta mention the solace of gettin' ta look at the lass on a daily basis," Palfrey added with a wink. When Nantze didn't answer for a while but just stared at the waning embers in front of him, Palfrey decided he needed to appeal to the man's compassionate side.

"Nantze, I'm tellin 'ya. If'n ya don't stay and intervene, that young lass there's goin' ta wither away ta nothin' an we'll be buryin' her dead, lifeless body next ta her mother!" Motioning with his hands in a wild and exaggerated fashion, the spry old fellow added, "Now, ya listen ta an ol' man. She is pinin' fer her family, and will join 'em, too, if'n she doesn't have somethin' ta live fer." As Palfrey spoke, the caterpillars on his brow drooped, making Nantze's heart fill with compassion for the pair of them.

"I know ya like the girl. If ya have a feelin' heart in ya, which I know ya do bein' a man what believes in God, you'll do what I tell ya. Accept the job then go ta the girl and tell her you're starvin' on yer own cookin', which is in all ways true, and that you'll gladly pay her if she'll fix ya yer meals every day!" he continued, a small tear clinging to his lashes before thundering out again. "The girl's got a heart of gold buried under all those quills, and here's what I says, she needs ta have someone who needs her. She's cared fer someone else her whole life and is lost. If'n ya can get her ta cook fer ya, ya can get her ta eat, too. I ain't never met a woman who dinna taste as she went along ta make sure her food dinna need somethin' extra like. And she sets a great store upon her house-keepin'." When Nantze still didn't say anything, Palfrey, with his emotions raging in his eyes, added, "You'll be savin' a life, man!

There's no higher callin' fer a man than that!"

Nantze, tearing up himself, tore his eyes away from Palfrey's forlorn face and replied, "Alright Palfrey, I'll give it a go," he began but added quickly, "That doesn't mean that I'm gonna stay over long. I don't fancy the idea everyone's got floatin' around in their skulls that I'm hungry fer the forge! I'm not! Of course, I won't say I don't fancy the lass." Smiling and shaking his head at the thought of the girl, Nantze went on, "She's a more beautiful sprite than I've ever seen! All fire and damnation one moment and lamb's wool and flower pedals the next!" Nantze's eyes, as Palfrey watched him, filled with the future regardless of what his words said, and the old man could see the boy was smitten.

"I knewed ya were the one, and don't worry about the men. The way they looked tonight, I thought a few of 'em were gonna shed a tear themselves! Beyond that, ya just get that fool girl ta start eatin' again and give her a task ta keep her occupied. Mind she's got a tongue o' fire, and she can spot a scheme a mile off, but she's every intention that ya should stay. The only snag is she says she's not ready ta feed ya."

"Well then, let's hope she changes her mind afore I wither away!"

Palfrey paused, elated. "I tell ya, she just needs a man ta take care of. That'll brin' her 'round. Once she has someone countin' on her, she'll have a purpose again. You'll see," Palfrey told him with an ear to ear grin as he repeatedly shook the miracle worker's hand, and his eyebrows broke out in song. Then whispering, Palfrey added, "I've already dropped a seed, mind. I let it slip I thought ya was lookin' puny. You just play up how yer feelin' sickly survivin' on yer own rank meals."

"I think I can manage it, seein' as I'm near starvin'!" Nantze whispered back before adding with a cocky, bright smile, "Besides that, I've a smooth set of manners with the ladies. She'll not see through me," he told the old man with a wink before he began to amble around the forge testing out his adjustments again.

Following him, Palfrey attempted to set him on his guard, "Well now, don't discount the girl entirely. She's not so easily ruffled as all that!" He tried to warn him as his blue eyes sparkled mischievously underneath a set of merry twin brows. "She's a keen one and mighty bright!" he emphasized dramatically, "and ya saw yerself how she waylaid those blokes today."

Smiling, Nantze shot him a knowing look. "I know how ta handle the woman," he told him with a wave of his hand as he thought of their conversation in the wagon earlier in the day and how he was able to humble her rather swiftly.

"I hope ya do, lad! I hope ya do," Palfrey finished up before he went in to tell Kate the good news.

Coming into the house after a short rap on the door, "Says he'll stay," the old man popped off, his eyebrows arched appropriately upwards.

"Ya coulda had some compassion on my poor nerves!" Kate let out with a pent up sigh, "I've been nearly ill waitin' fer ya ta return!" the girl huffed, "Thought maybe I offended him the other day, or mayhap it wouldn't be enough ta drag him away from the railroad."

"Seems he likes the idea of workin' fer himself. Told 'em he'd be a slave if'n he decided ta take the job with the railroad. No doubt they'd have the man runnin' hither and yon at the drop of hat, and him with that bum leg."

"What about his work in Lancaster?"

"Likes the idea of workin' at his own pace."

"What of the meals? What'd he say ta that?"

"Only that if'n he couldn't manage, he'd go back ta Lancaster and Mrs. Wilmarth's cookin'. Said it wouldn't do him a drop o' good ta make more money and work less hours if'n he starved ta death," Palfrey told her in hopes that she'd be afraid to lose him over something as trifling as three meals a day, and from the looks of her in the waning fire light, Palfrey could see that losing him was a real concern for the girl.

DAINA LAND

∞ ∞ ∞

Chapter Nine

The next evening after having finally finished his work, Nantze hobbled up from the smithy shop to the well before going to tap on Katie's front door with the bridge of his somewhat still sooty knuckles. A cocky little set of his chin was just barely perceptible beneath the thick-stubble of his whiskers.

After cleaning himself up for dinner at the Sow, he rambled up to the cottage. Perhaps she would recognize now, after having talked to Palfrey, that he had some options available to him if she chose not to feed him. There was just no plausible reason for him to dine at the Sow every evening. He could do it, of course, but having to take himself off every night in search of a meal zapped what little energy he had left off a night.

When he tapped on her door, Katie rose from her place in her father's chair before the fire. It was not quite dark out but too dark to see clearly inside the house. Still she hadn't bothered to get up to light the lamp. In fact, she'd noticed Nantze had stopped hammering a while ago. She knew she should have been preparing herself a meal but found she had no appetite.

Hearing a tap again and looking out the slim line of the decorated window frame, Katie could see the outline of her new smithy and sighed. She had no desire to talk to him today of all days.

"Katie," he began when she answered his knock. "May I come in?"

She said nothing but backed away from the door as he made his way inside the kitchen. She looked pale and depressed. Had Nantze known when the Cinnies had died, he'd have known that today had been two months since the accident, and Kate was feeling the anniversary of her loss keenly.

When she didn't offer him a seat, he coughed into his hand and cleared his throat. "Been on my bum leg a bit too long, mind if I sit down fer a piece?" he asked, hoping it would instill compassion.

It didn't.

When she cut a sideways glance at him, he became a little harried, so he spurted out as he hobbled to a kitchen chair, "I won't be long about my request, Kate."

However, so far, nothing was going as smoothly as it had when he'd practiced his speech repeatedly throughout the day as he pounded away on one piece of iron after another. Each ping accented his words as he had rehearsed them to pass the day. Not that he had any reserves about his ability after so many milestones between them. Besides that, he knew he was a handsome man, and felt that after their talk the other day, he knew how to deal with the girl; therefore, he forged ahead regardless of the pallid look of her skin and the pursed lines around her lips.

"As ya know, the work of a smithy requires stamina, which is somethin' I canna keep up survivin' as I am on my own measly grub and stew at the Sow. By the time I get there every night, I'm near starved and fall on the food so fast I barely chew. In short, I need better meals than I can provide fer myself." Here he stopped to gather breath and contort his face slightly in an effort to look needy and try to play upon the lady's sympathies before continuing.

"Would ya be willin' ta prepare me an egg or two?" Thinking about his normal breakfast meals, he added, "Perhaps more and some meat and bread in the morning, a hearty meal of nights, and a bit of a sturdy lunch containin' some kind of meat each meal?" When she didn't respond, he stopped to think of what else he could say. "I'll buy whatever ya need, of course," he added with his hands raised. When she still only looked blankly at him, he added, "And gladly pay ya fer yer efforts. Or if'n ya'd rather, ya can deduct what seems right ta ya from my pay."

He then smiled at her as he knew made most girls sweeten up to him and waited for it to have the same effect on her. It didn't.

So he waited.

And waited.

Until finally a look of suspicion and unbelief overtook her countenance. "Where do ya plan on eatin' these meals?" she asked coldly.

Caught off guard by her change in personality since yesterday, he became nervous. "Out in the shop," he answered with haste, melting under her scrutiny. "I won't be botherin' ya in any case," he added.

Then regrouping the smooth set of manners he told Palfrey he possessed, he added, "It would simply just be a shame ta have lived through the horrors of war only ta die from eatin' my own grub, now wouldn't it?" His joke didn't produce the smile he expected. So he offered, what he assumed, was another stunning smile. Kate, instead of smiling back, only lowered her gaze and scrutinized him more harshly.

"Must be an off day for me," he told himself when she was still totally unaffected by the charm that usually held him in good standing with the ladies. When she finally did speak, he almost jumped.

"I won't be cookin' food I canna eat, and you'll have ta make do with whatever I decide ta do. No complaining. No requests. Ya'd get milk, cheese, bread, and hot soup or stew or whatever meat I make. I'd do it just as I—just as..." she paused. "Just as I've always done, and that's only if'n I accept. So don't be lettin' in any fool ideas that I'm agreein' yet," she told him when she saw a glint of pride in his eyes, signifying he felt like he'd made a conquest.

"And until I'm ready, ya'd have ta go ta market on Mondays afore ya begin yer work. I'd send ya with a list. You'd be payin' fer both of us eat," she announced. "Not that I'm eatin' much anyway.

I don't have the stomach fer it!"

Her rapid-shot words peppered the conversation, revealing the fire in her blood. He was pleased because she was going to need it in the weeks and months ahead, but like the other men who knew her, he was learning to have a healthy fear of the little thing. What was most surprising was how much more fierce she was today. All blunt objects and no soft edges.

Then a new thought dawned in her head and streamed out her eyes, transforming her face again. "This don't mean anythin'. It doesn't make us... well, ya know...sweethearts. It doesn't mean we're courtin'. I won't be havin' the town's people waggin' their lips while I'm in mournin'," she popped off, waylaying him again.

"No! No," he told her, waving his hand for emphasis. "I'll not presume upon ya in any way. I promise. I'll gather my grub, return ta the forge, and not bother ya till the next mean...meal, next meal," he stammered; his hands still raised.

Glaring at him with the same look that proceeded every fiery question, she lifted her chin. "Why didn't ya ask Ivy, Palfrey's wife? She'd have taken care of ya." Katie asked as she crossed her arms and sized him up, searching his face for any other motives. She knew her smithy shop would be a fine dowry prize, and after having had time to think about their conversation the other day, she realized the man could say anything he liked. It didn't mean he meant it.

"Ivy?" he began, thinking up a quick return. "Now, what kind of man do ya take me fer?" he asked, putting his hand on his heart as if he were offended. "Doesn't she have enough ta do just keepin' up with Palfrey?" Expecting her to waylay him or tell him to eat at the Sow, he squinted to deflect the next set of rounds he was anticipating.

But they didn't come, instead Katie smiled but only slightly. "Aye, she does at that!" she returned, thinking of the old codger and relaxing her stance just slightly by lowering her crossed arms away from the seat of her hurt—her heart.

When she smiled, even as slightly as it was, something in Nantze lurched, and he had to ask himself just who that scheming old devil, Palfrey, was trying to save—him—or—her?

Finally, after much deliberation, she agreed. Still, Nantze held back his smile. She was not in the mood nor easily fooled. And he didn't want to lose the ground he'd gained, so he simply nodded in response and took his leave. The tiny little girl had spirit, and he was beginning to admire her—immensely, which made him want to rethink his stance on leaving, too.

Palfrey had been waiting in the forge for Nantze when he got back.

"Did it work?"

"Yes, Palfrey, it did. She'll do it," Nantze began.

"Now, there boy, don't ya go gettin' cocky. Like I said, she's a fiery lass. You have ta move with care, boy!

"I can easily see that!" Nantze exclaimed, "She'd have been a great help in the war!" His words, bursting out a little too loudly, made Palfrey raise and lower his hands to shush him before stealing a look up to the house to see if Kate was on the porch and had heard him.

"Now, don't go givin' me away ya fool. She'll know we've been schemin' somethin' if she finds us together."

Taking his cue, Nantze lowered his voice. "She's in strange form tonight. I tell ya, that girl spits words, reloads, and fires with amazin' speed and accuracy." Then, wanting to get the old man riled, he added, "You could have warned me!"

At that statement, the old man's twin caterpillars arched upward in offended surprise. "And this from a man just back from war! I hadn't known I was sendin' in a coward!"

"A coward ya say!" the invalid counter as he leapt toward the old man. "I'll show ya my cowardice! Prepare yourself, ya swine!"

Soon both men had armed themselves with metalwork from around the forge. One lunged while the other parried. The clang being clearly heard in the house. As one was old and the other lame, they made a fitting pair—an even match. Each giving a good showing of himself, the excitement of the exercise built to a frenzied height but was instantly deflated when both sighted the small figure standing just outside the forge with her hands planted firmly on her thin hips and flanked by both the dog and cat.

Although the woman held her tongue, which was a novelty under the circumstances, the men, having been caught fencing with makeshift swords, both paused, offered an embarrassed, shy smile, and put their weapons upon the nearest level surface. Katie, after seeing their foolishness, hemmed, shook her head at their juvenile games, turned her back, and strode purposefully back to the house amid her furry entourage with a small smile lifting the corners of her pursed lips and a light shining pleasantly from her previously stern eyes.

Once her back was turned, the men looked at one another, a mischievous smile pasted upon their guilty countenances, and bowed slightly from the waist. Both, acknowledging to the other, they had met their match. The old man, happy with the current circumstances, danced himself off to the Sow before going home to tell Ivy the good news. On the other hand, Nantze, turned on his heel and attempted to bound up to the loft; however, his excited movements, regardless of how simple, somehow always felt more like a strange heathen dancing ritual, and since his contraption clanked and groaned, every bodily movement seemed accompanied by an embarrassing ting.

∞∞∞

Chapter Ten

When morning dawned, Nantze was up and stoking the fire. His stump had been raw ever since setting the fence and had finally cracked from the exertion of his sword fight the night before, so he decided not to attach his leg. Instead he covered the stump with salve, and tucked his pant leg into the back pocket of his trousers, making sure to let the sore get some air. Although uncommon, it certainly wasn't the first time it split open, and he knew more than anyone that he had to be careful, of course. Infection was a horrible and real fear for a man in his position.

When he heard Katie shuffling around in the house, he pulled a canvas bag over one shoulder, filled it with wood, and teetered on his crutches to the door. Tapping lightly and removing the bag, he left it, grabbed a pail from a nail on the porch, and limped off to the pump. By the time he got back to the house, half of the contents had slopped out.

"Maybe she'd be better off gatherin' the water herself," he thought to himself. The thing of it was, he wanted her to know that he was willing to be helpful. Fetching the water was a woman's job, but he hoped it made him look humble. It was hard to tell how'd she'd take it though. She was shrewd.

After hearing him, she went to the door. Expecting her to be pleased with his goodwill offering, Nantze was surprised when she barked, "Where's yer leg?"

"Thought I'd let the stump get some air."

"Hurt yerself last night, dinna ya?" Shocked by her question, he attempted to play it off as something that was somewhat common, so he shrugged.

"Hmmph, yer food's ready." Standing at the door to get his plate, Nantze waited until she brought it to him.

"Thought ya'd might as well eat at the table," she began and left the door open for him to come in. "Won't do ta have ya wobblin' back with the plate later. Might as well just let me wash it as soon as yer done as wait 'til the food's dried ta the plate, and I have ta scrub it."

"Yes, mam," Nantze answered rather surprised at her. She was a striking little thing. Her abundant dark hair and complexion accented her fiery blue-green eyes and on occasion, when she let her guard down for a moment, small dimples played at the corners of her smile.

Laying by the fire, the large, wiry-haired hound stretched out and yawned. Katie stepped to his dish and cracked an egg into it, patted his head, and explained, "Eggs are good fer his coat."

"Ya know, I've never asked his name?"

"Gauche."

Knowing it meant graceless, Nantze offered. "You might very well call me the same!"

"I might if ya don't take care of that leg!" she shot back, obviously irritated by the thought that he was hurt.

"I'll be fine in a day or two."

However, when Nantze wobbled up on the third day without his contraption, Katie took matters into her own hands. As Nantze was finishing up his eggs, she took down her hair and began to brush it. The length of it reached down past her buttock. Nantze, not wanting to seem enthralled, stood and carried his plate to the sink.

As she brushed out her hair, she spoke, "Ya won't be workin' the bellows this mornin' Nantze."

"Do ya need me ta go into town?"

"No," she told him as she began to create a thick dark braid. Her fingers worked nimbly and within the short span of three held breaths, Nantze was surprised to find he could breathe again. Her beauty, as the men in the neighborhood knew, was uncommon, and having taken down the braid she'd been wearing during her period of mourning, the little lady resembled an enchantress. Her dress, which in most cases would have been black, was not. She hadn't time to sew herself all of her mourning clothes yet, so on this day her dress was a lovely sky blue. She had, however, wrapped a black shawl around her shoulders, which she tucked into her skirt, and had wound a thick, black-silk ribbon through her hair. It lay discarded on the kitchen table next to the hairbrush until she used it again to tie her braid.

Next, as Nantze watched, she went to the cupboard and took down the whiskey. From another cupboard she pulled out a brown salve. What she did next, however, nearly made the man swoon. Pulling out the cork with her teeth and handing him the bottle, a look of pure compassion converted her darling little face and transforming her, in his opinion, to the exact representation of an angelic host, she said, "Drink this and do it with all speed!" Once the bottle was up to his lips, she added, "and take down yer pants!"

Spurting out the contents of his mouth, Nantze asked, "What?"

"You heard me! Take down yer pants!"

"Katie?"

"Ya,"

"What ya plannin' on doin' here, Kate?"

"Somethin' ya won't like at all until perhaps next week," she answered back.

"Really, woman, my leg's not that bad!"

"Take down yer pants!" she barked again, "or I'll be doin' it myself!"

How she knew his leg had gotten as bad as it was, Nantze had no idea, but he knew if something wasn't done and done soon, the oozing puss spilling out from his stump was going to become a serious threat.

Looking over at the salve and bowl of steaming water filled with herbs the woman had organized on the table, seeing the look of determination upon her face, and taking a few more swigs of good Scottish whiskey to fortify himself, Nantze pulled down his trousers, kicked them off of his ankle, and sat back down.

Examining the wound, Katie replied, "I've seen worse!" Then pulling up her skirts and flipping her braid to hang down the length of her back, she took a seat in his lap with her back facing his face, grabbed up his stump, and told him to bite down on her braid, "HARD!"

"Bite on yer braid?" he squeaked out in confusion.

"Screw yer courage ta the stickin' place, man!" she offered with an upraised fist and a nod of assurance, making Nantze grin.

Grabbing up his face between both her small hands, she looked him in the eyes. "Although I don't know ya so well, I know I couldn't handle it if ya died from a wound on yer leg when I coulda saved ya!" Then with a compassion he had not seen in her before, she turned around to face him, grabbed up her braid, shoved it in his mouth, and pulled his arms around her waist. "Rest yer head upon my back," she whispered, and surprisingly he did what he was told.

Screwing up more than his courage, he braced himself for what he knew was coming. The Lord knew how many such treatments he'd received. Cleaning a wound of this sort was anything but pleasant. Having a beautiful woman on his lap was new, and more importantly, it was a great solace, and before he knew it, he had his arms wrapped around her tiny waist and was biting down on her braid as she'd instructed him.

First she covered his stump with a towel soaked in the hot water and herbs to release the infection and then squeezed out the puss. Next she opened the wound's mouth and ladled in the herbal water numerous times, then to his horror, doused it with the whiskey. During the whole of this portion of the operation, Nantze was thankful for the braid. He'd not stopped chomping on the thing yet.

"Ya alright? Ya wanna a bit of a moment or shall I just get it done?" she asked, turning around to face him and bringing their faces only inches apart.

Grunting out his words, Nantze asked for the bottle. After a few more swigs and time enough for it to settle his nerves, he bravely cried out, "Go on!"

With his permission, she shoved in a healthy portion of propolis salve and wrapped the stump in a clean herb-soaked cloth. Feeling keenly his weakness and wishing she could aid him, she climbed off his lap, turned to face him, kissed his stubbled-cheek, and helped him to her father's chair. Once situated, she hoisted his stump, put it on the stool, and carefully placed a pillow under it. Then pushing on top of the chair, she leaned it back to make him more comfortable, retrieved the whiskey from the kitchen table, placed it on a chairside chest, and left him alone to rest.

"All I need now is that cat!" he called out with a grin when she began to tidy up the kitchen.

"Mind yerself, or I'll oblige ya!" This time when she smiled, her whole face brightened and her eyes sparkled mischievously, making Nantze's heart lurch and realize his error.

"Kate!" Nantze called after some quiet reflection. She, however, had left the room and gone somewhere into the environs of the stately old cottage, and when she didn't come, he called out more fiercely, "KATE!"

"What is it?" Running into the room, she threw down the pillow and blanket she was carrying and placed a hand on his forehead then checked his wound. "Are ya feelin' feverish? Ya have a chill?" she fired off so quickly Nantze couldn't speak his mind. "Oh, it's the pain, isn't it? It's peaked! I'll get the laudanum and make a cordial!" she cried out flustered and turned, rushing amid a swirl of skirts and nerves.

Grabbing up her hand as she tried to spin away, Nantze whispered, "Stop!"

Kate stared down at him. His eyes were shining and a peaceful countenance rested upon him, making her realize he had something significant to say, so she stopped and gave him her full attention.

"I lied ta ya, Kate!" Nantze told her, holding her hand in his and playing lightly with her fingers. "I told ya…"

Interrupting his confession and attempting to snatch away her hand, Kate's eyes filled with the instantaneous fire he'd come to admire so much in her. "I knew I shouldn't of trusted ya!"

"Let me finish woman!" Nantze began again, his hand grabbing out and clasping down upon hers to keep her from running off again. Feeling exhausted, he exhaled. "Yer always interruptin' a man!"

"Fine! What grand lie did ya tell me?" she asked, drawing out the word grand, rolling her eyes, and shaking her head in disgust. Then thinking of something else, she added, "And be quick about it will ya. I've not all day ta listen ta yer squabble! It's washin' day, and I've the beddin' ta air! Dinner ta make, of course, and…"

Pulling down on her arm and sitting up at the same time, Nantze, with a gentle smile, lovingly took her chin in his hand and tried to shush her; however, the force of those quick movements brought the thick braid of her hair flying around her shoulder, and it being as equally offended as Kate was herself, slapped him in the cheek.

Closing his eyes and exhaling loudly, he tried again. And again his brown eyes softened, but this time when he spoke, his voice was filled with a vibrant energy she'd not heard him use before. "I lied," he paused a moment as a wave of gentle compassion crossed his features, "when I said I dinna want a wife." Here he paused to watch her and let the meaning of his words soak in.

When her eyes registered understanding, he added, "I do! I want a wife! I want a tiny fire-sprite of a wife, who throws out words like darts, who's one minute all pedals and rosebuds and the next fire and rough edges. I want a wife who can take a man's middles and turn them ta mush just by smilin' at him."

Shocked speechless, which was a small miracle in its own right, Kate could only stare at him a moment. "Ya want a wife who's all needles and thorns?"

"I do, Kate!" he added, caressing her flushed cheek.

Standing quickly and pointing to her black shawl, she cried out, "I canna marry ya! I'm in mournin'!"

Shaking his head and pinching the bridge of his nose at her swift moving thoughts, he reminded her in his quiet gentle way, "I haven't asked ya yet, Kate!"

"Oh!" she answered and shook her head. Her long dark braid swishing back and forth from the movement. "Right!" she began then smiled and nodded her head in understanding. However, as he watched her, the fire, he'd become accustomed to seeing when she thought of something new to say, returned to her bright eyes, and she pointed at his chest, "Ya still have ta woo me!"

Breaking out in a boisterous laugh, Nantze pulled the girl down on his lap and planted a sweet kiss on her sweeter lips. "I've every intention, sweetheart!"

Having been busy when her visitor arrived, Kate hadn't noticed Palfrey pressing his nose to the glass pane of her front door. Had she looked up, she would have seen his twin caterpillar brows arched in excited surprise and blue fire crackle out of his bluer eyes.

He'd come, of course, to check on Nantze and see how he was getting on with the girl. Not finding him in the shop nor seeing the fire even so much as stoked, he ambled up to the porch to catch the man at his morning meal; however, seeing Kate on his lap wrestling his stump clean and Nantze with his arms around her waist and a look of excruciating pain maligning his features, the old duffer, with his nose still pressed to the glass, was as excited as a child on Christmas morning. To attest to this fact and give praise where it was due, Palfrey's animated eyebrows stood and gave testimonials prior to joining hands and singing a harmonic rendition of the hallelujah chorus as it was obvious, even to them, that a notable miracle had taken place.

Equally surprising was Palfrey's response. In fact, had anyone seen him as he hurried his limber limbs down the small hamlet road, they would have undoubtedly wondered what in that unpleasant scenario had pleased him so profusely, and if he were asked why, one would think he would have an extremely difficult time explaining his adulation over learning about Nantze's worrisome infection and Katie's unconventional care of it.

To further stupefy his neighbors, those traveling along the cart road that morning saw the old man whistle a jig and spryly jump up to tap his heels together before turning his happy stride in the direction of the Yellow Sow to let go the happy news of Katie's impending vows. Thereby dispelling the town people's fears that she would run off the new smithy, or worse, join the rest of her family.

Thank you for purchasing this book. It is my goal to create a novel that is enjoyable to read, well edited, and respectful of the time and money you have invested in me. If you feel I have honored your expectations, I ask that you leave a review, so that others who like the same genre will have the benefit of your opinion.

∞ ∞ ∞

About the Author

Daina Land's love of British romances began with the Regency Romance classics. Since then she has devoted her creative efforts to writing romances primarily set in England. She currently resides in Texas with her husband, Tim and their children. She is an English teacher specializing in writing and works as a teacher consultant for the East Texas Writing Project. She has presented creative writing workshops for young writers, education professionals, and college students. She writes novels, novellas, poetry, children's books, and short stories.

∞ ∞ ∞

Connect with Me

I'd love to hear from you. As a teacher of writing, my passion is educating students of all ages. For tips on revising and editing, grammar, and writing prompts, please follow me on Facebook or email me at dainalandwrites@gmail.com

Coming July 30, 2020

The Runaway Betrothal

Having lived through the outbreaks of cholera, the horrors of the battlefield, and the questionable cleanliness of the Barrack Hospital in Scutari near Istanbul as he recovered from losing his leg during the Crimean War, Nantze turns to helping others as a way to overcome his injuries. Once able to hobble around, the gentle spoken man with the gift of encouragement uses his knowledge as a blacksmith to make himself a mechanical leg. When he starts making them for other men in the amputee ward, he's instantly hailed as a miracle worker.

Finding herself bereft of her brother and father and in need of a blacksmith to run the shop their deaths left behind, Katie Christison, a quick tempered beauty known for speaking her mind, is forced to choose between hiring a man to work the bellows and succumbing to her overwhelming feelings of loss.

Seeing that Kate prefers the latter, a group of her father's friends intervene on her behalf and advertise for a blacksmith, but with Kate's sharp tongue and fiery temper, they are all left wondering whether Nantze can live up to his name and somehow forge together the pieces of Kate's broken heart before she succeeds in running him off.

∞ ∞ ∞

A sample chapter is included in this book. It is my express wish that you will enjoy reading it as much as I have enjoyed writing it.

The Runaway Betrothal
Daina Land

CHAPTER ONE

∞ ∞ ∞

Sitting haphazardly upon a too small stool in the comfort of his own elaborate establishment in London, Ichabod Hasting scratched out orders on high quality parchment, whose header in large, bold script read, East India Trading Company. Under the header, resided his name. Once finished, this parchment was stuffed into a package along with eight letters to varied individuals with whom he was acquainted. Each letter, written in the same style, upon the same high quality paper, and closed with the same officious wax seal of crimson, carried with it a series of directions, instructions, and, if one cared for the comments of the receivers of these letters, which, of course, Hasting did not, some remarkably high-handed demands.

Once all was made secure, the package, having already received its directions, was handed into the careful hands of a scruffy, sea-weathered gent, whose job, according to Hasting's specific criteria, was to carry it with him on his ship bound for Calcutta and to follow the directions precisely as they were written.

∞ ∞ ∞

In Kent, after some months' travel, the first of Hasting's letters lay officious-looking upon a stack of varied colored envelopes and invitations addressed to Ester O'Duncy. Essie to those who knew her, and the only sibling of the letter's author, Icky Hasting.

"Drood! Drood! Good gracious man! Where are you?" O'Duncy screeched as she fluttered around the room in her immaculate morning gown of rose gold. Her stays, moaning under the pressure of such quick and uncharacteristic action, were no hindrance to her speedy thoughts and piercing tongue.

"Madam?" Drood asked in monotone syllables while entering the fashionable salon as fast as a man of his age, income, and station would permit himself to go. Having been many years in the lady's employ and having lived as a child on her father's estate, he was never much moved by her freaks of temperament and instead traversed through the world at a stately, even pace.

"Prepare the carriage! I must be off to Brighton!" she squawked awkwardly.

"And when shall you be leaving, mam?" Drood asked unmoved.

"As soon as may be!" she heaved, holding her hand to her ample bosom.

"Of course," Drood answered with a respectful bow before thinking it incumbent of him to ask, "And will I be going with you?"

"Yes," she began as she fluttered around her lovely room of sedate, dove grey hues. Her mind clearing to the idea of her quick departure, she added, "and Peck, of course." Pausing again, she continued, "and George. He can always be depended upon as can you, Drood!" she added, patting the man's hand in an uncharacteristic show of emotion. When Drood tarried momentarily taken aback by her kind retort, O'Duncy squawked, "Well, make haste, man! We must be off!"

"As you wish it, mam," he added with a slight almost imperceptible smile and a nod before removing himself from the room to prepare the household and himself for their departure.

Once Drood exited, the good lady looked again at the letter from her brother. "There now old girl! Get thee to the Old Ship in Brighton double quick. The game's afoot!" She read with some great agitation before pulling the bell chord for a servant and muttering her strong displeasure at being uprooted so suddenly on what she hoped was not another of Icky's slick tricks. It was just like her fidgety brother to put forth some wild scheme without so much as a vague reference to his plan. She had learned over the years, however, to trust his quirks and freaks. This strange affair, however, involved his only daughter, Elinore, thus it put her blood up.

"Oh my," she fretted again as she waited on a maid. Her hands, in a twitter of nerves, fidgeted at her throat one moment and patted her hair the next until her nervous energy agitated her into motion. Finally settling on pacing the floor, she went first to her writing desk to start a list then moved across the room to gaze lovingly over the immaculate grounds of the estate and curse Icky under her breath as a heathen.

"I should have pushed him out of that tree when I'd had the chance!" She decided as she thought about all the scrapes he'd gotten her into over the years. As she fluttered, her anxious energy finally found an outlet in devising ways to best torture her brother when next they met. Currently the lady's ideas rattled between boxing his ears and planting him a five-fingered-facer.

"Leastwise, that is what I think it's called these days," she mused. "Regardless, I should take great pleasure in giving him a bit of his own back!" Imagining her small fist connecting with her brother's rather bulbous nose helped abate a small portion of her angst, so she continued her rant with more pleasure than was expected in a woman of her age and breeding.

"Run me all across the globe, indeed!" she huffed before reading the vague contents of his letter again. With her curiosity piqued, as Icky knew it would be, Essie attempted to unravel what precisely he meant by writing, "I have the bride, the dowry, and the groom. Now it's up to you to make the wedding!"

"Mam?" a homely girl asked with a bow, interrupting Lady O'Duncy's thoughts.

"Yes," she announced upon seeing her. "Go speak to Peck, and between the two of you, pack my things. I've decided to spend some weeks in Brighton with my good friends. I've mentioned them, I'm sure, Donne, Cowper, and Moody," the good lady told the girl in what she hoped sounded like her natural tenor. Her voice, however, seemed unnaturally high-pitched even to her own ears.

The abigail, being newly hired and not used to such goings-ons, bowed to her mistress and set out straight away to do as she was bid, all fidgets and strife. In her lady's room, the young maid informed Peck, her lady's personal attendant, to gather such things as she expected her lady to need. The frazzled girl then made a few inquiries as to Peck's wishes and spent the remainder of the day organizing, packing, and alternately repacking Lady O'Duncy's trunks for a summer holiday at the seaside with Peck constantly fussing at her about how best to do the business.

O'Duncy, on the other hand, spent her time nervously pouring over engagements that needed canceling, adding names to a list, and putting together the estimated figures she expected her brother, Ichabod Hasting, would desire an account of should this, his latest scheme, come to fruition.

∞∞∞

In London, the second letter arrived at the establishment of *Gimley and Gimley* where Gimley the Lesser stood riveted to his desk with Hasting's letter gripped tightly between thumb and fingers. "Get the Hasting file!" he demanded of his underling. Once received, that man scanned documents long since kept buried. "Bring me the item housed in section 118-5 and be quick about it you fool!" he yelled at the man.

"Sir?" his attendant asked, knowing that the owner of that item had not contacted the firm in years.

"I have need of it!" Gimley the Lesser yelled before calling for his father, the senior Gimley of *Gimley and Gimley*. When that aged gentleman finally shuffled into his son's office, he was in no humor to be further agitated.

"What's all this hullabaloo, Junior?" Gimley senior grumbled at his fidgeting son.

"Only this," Gimley the Lesser began, holding up an officious looking paper, "a letter from Hasting!" Making quick, jerky steps, Gimley the Lesser moved to where his father stood and shook the paper very near the old man's nose.

"Don't be impertinent!" his father barked, grabbing hold of the letter and reading Hasting's scrawl for himself. "When did this arrive?" the old man continued, eyes ogling from sunken sockets. After shaking his head at his son's obvious ignorance then double checking the date on the missive, he peered at his watch. "What is today's date?" the elder grumbled much peeved.

"The twenty-first and my boy brought it from the sorting house just a few hours hence."

"And you are just now showing it to me? Ignorant boy! What preparations have you made?"

"None, sir. I, too, have only just read the letter myself and have come to you straight away," his son told him in defense of his actions.

"Well, there's nothing for it! You must get to White's and seek this," here the greater Gimley paused and looked back at the epistle to reacquaint himself with the man's name written there, "seek out this man, Engle, and give him what Hasting requires!"

"Yes," replied his son in shocked remonstration, "but we've not heard from Hasting in years! What makes you believe this document is genuine? Perhaps it is some ploy. It may be an elaborate heist of some sort."

"I've told you before not to read those damn penny novels! They fill your head with rot! No one has known the whereabouts of that item for these twenty years and more. In fact, I rather doubt this man Engle even knows its value. Besides that, if you weren't as daft as a duffer, you'd have looked in his file and seen the man's scrawl for yourself!"

"I've already called for his file!" His son told him much offended before walking the short distance to his desk, grabbing the file, and returning to his father's side. "The handwriting looks genuine," replied the son as the two inspected the letter.

"It's Hasting's alright!" then looking at his son he added, "What are you about, you fool! You must change! You cannot go to White's looking like a solicitor!" Gazing down at his normal garb, Gimley the Lesser brushed off a bit of white lint from his sleeve before excusing himself in a twitter of nerves. Although his father thought nothing of highwaymen in the city of London, he certainly did.

Therefore, after his father shuffled out of the room and prior to his making any other arrangements, he returned to his desk, bent down to click a small release switch under the center drawer, and pulled out an aged, painted tin box from its hiding place. Opening it revealed a matched set of small dueling pistols. Checking them over and reaching down again into the hidden compartment, he pulled out a handful of bullets, placed them in the guns, snapped them shut, and shoved them down into opposite pockets of his drab, black coat.

Having already spoken privately to his driver prior to his entering the carriage and having given him instructions for their progress across town, he commanded him to keep a sharp eye on the goings-on of other rigs. After that, he alighted the carriage steps, scrambled inside to rest his nerves on the well-oiled leather seats, and pulled a lap robe over his bony knees. Once settled, he rapped on the roof of the carriage with the handle of his umbrella, signaling his desire to depart.

Knowing Gimley the Lesser's propensity to overreact to unexpected stimuli, his driver, a man named John, weaving the carriage through London's side streets, finally deposited his passenger on the steps of the Gimley family home.

Dislodging himself from the carriage with his driver's assistance, he mounted the steps and strode with purposeful strides into the large foyer amid the shock and stares of his father's household staff. Waving away first the butler's then the housekeeper's questioning looks, he ascended the ornate center staircase to his own rooms where he disrobed, washed, and dressed himself in his best attire.

Once all was made as elegant as he had the ability to contrive on such a strict budget as his father demanded, Gimley the Lesser made his way to White's in the same fashion as he had made his way home, which included no less than three unnecessary right turns, a series of erratic weaving between carriages and donkey carts, and a number of side streets.

Having finally pulled up in front of the posh men's club, checking again to make sure that the item he was to deliver was still housed within the confines of the ornate container, and patting his pockets to reassure himself he still had the dueling pistols, he lifted up a silent prayer that the recipient would be in residency.

He had not the stamina to reenact this horrid scenario on another occasion; therefore, uncovering his knobby knees and waiting for his driver to open the carriage door so that he might extricate himself from the confines of the rig, Gimley anxiously looked around before stepping down.

"Anything untoward?" he asked John.

"No, sir," the man nervously replied.

"No one's followed us?" Gimley asked his voice edged, beads of sweat gathered on his brow, and the hairs of his neck standing at attention. "You're certain?"

"Yes, sir!"

"Very well. If I am not out within a quarter of an hour, come look for me!" Gimley told his man. "And bring this with you!" he added, placing one of the loaded pistols in the man's grasp.

Looking down into his hand, his driver croaked in surprise. "Of course, sir, but I cannot think this will be necessary?"

"One never knows what a derelict individual or hardened criminal might think to do!" he told John with a defining nod.

Then feeling again in his pocket for the box, wrapping his sweaty fist around it, and patting his own small firearm, he made his way up the steps of White's.

∞∞∞

Finally landing, on British soil and making his way to his London club, Liles Engle, a gentleman employee and underling of Hasting's division of the *East India Trading Company*, walked into White's to enjoy his respite. As was expected of those frequenting the establishment, Liles was dressed in the posh style of a fashionable man.

Finding a relaxing spot from where he might enjoy watching the foot traffic, Liles sat down, stretched his long, athletic legs, clad in trousers of charcoal grey, comfortably in front of him, and determined to while away the remainder of the afternoon at his leisure by reading a good book; therefore, in an effort to make himself more comfortable by loosening slightly the intricately tied cravat at his throat and pulling somewhat at the wrists of his navy coat of superfine, which his tailor had expertly made to mold to his broad shoulders, he brushed aside a small fleck from his highly polished Hessians and crossed his feet.

An attendant, after asking about his health, informed him that a letter had arrived postmarked from Calcutta. An event, which although not uncommon, caused more than a little stir, considering the recipient had not been in attendance for over a year.

"I was away on business," Engle informed the man blandly, his grey eyes scanning the proffered envelope being held out to him.

"Just so," was that man's dry reply.

Removing his hat and gloves, placing them atop the table, and brushing aside a thick lock of dark hair, Liles, recognizing Hasting's seal, said, "Your best sherry, please."

"As you wish, sir," Liles heard before the attendant bowed.

As soon as that fellow's retreating foot falls could be heard padding away, he ripped along the edge of the envelope. Expecting to be informed about his wages and told to enjoy his holiday, Engle found himself surprised by the content of Hasting's letter.

As he read, he was emphatically commanded to seek out a room at an inn that had been reserved for him in Brighton. "Off you go! You'll be putting up at the Old Ship. Wait there for a man by the name of Quibbs. He will make arrangements for someone to take you in my carriage to look at a collection of Rockingham. An impressive AND inexpensive collection of Rockingham, I might add. The fellow, a gentleman by the name of Whitmore, has fallen on hard times and is desirous, as you can imagine, of parting with it at a bargain price, making your visit to him, excessively important. If it were not, I would not press you.

"I expect you will want to return to your own humble estate, Hertfordshire if I recall, for a day or two, but do not tarry overlong, eh? Also, get that man of yours, Jim, to travel to Hove and visit a fellow named Burls while you are there. His stock of horse flesh is considered the best in England."

While Liles processed this very unwelcome piece of news and Hasting's attempt at making it more palatable by suggesting he use the visit to restock his stables, a man, completely unknown to him, boldly made his way to his small table after having been motioned there by the attendant.

"Sir," the unknown fellow hemmed uncomfortably in front of Liles before boldly taking a seat across from him, knowing full-well that his actions broke the laws of gentlemanly etiquette upheld at such an establishment. Still the job must be done, and he, according to his father, was the only one to do it.

"May I be of service to you, sir?" was Engle's somewhat surprised reply as he faced the man, who was, as anyone could see, out of his element and uncomfortable about it.

"You Engle?" the thin, little man asked in obvious discomfiture, sweat hanging upon his upper lip and a nervous looking twitch playing across the recesses of his brow.

"I am," Engle answered much perplexed by the array of strange events.

"Then put this in your pocket," the man commanded, looking

nervously around at the other patrons in White's and sliding a publication of little importance across the table.

"What is it?" Liles asked, opening the periodical slightly and looking down at the ornately decorated case hidden within the folds of the magazine.

To this, however, the man had no response. Instead he replied, "Ichabod sent it. Said you'd take care of it for him, and that I was to tell you to take it with you when you go to Whitmore's!"

"Who are you?" Liles asked as he slyly slipped the box down into the pocket of his coat without looking at it.

"His banker. Watch yourself. You don't want a popper like that to go missing, nor someone to get wind of its value!" was all the man said before looking Liles directly in the eye, nodding, and patting the pistol in his coat pocket to insinuate that he had taken every precaution and so should Engle.

While the slick little man was still patting his pocket, the attendant returned with a tray, hemmed politely, and silently placed the snifter of sherry upon the table before quietly walking away.

Seeing it and feeling the need for fortification, Gimley's junior partner, snatched it up and slapped it back. Once the glass was empty, he plopped it down on the table with a thud, stood, nodded to Engle like a man pleased to have passed off a horrid piece of business, told him to mind he knew where it was at all times, and departed, eyes darting and visibly shaken.

Liles, dumbfounded by the man's strange behavior and intrigued by his even stranger talk, took out the box, hid it under the lip of the table, and looked in. After having ogled the item for some few seconds and in an effort to be certain he knew what his employer was commanding, he closed it again, lifted his hand to the attendant for a refill, and read and re-read the letter he'd received when he arrived.

He could neither, however, surmise a reason for that gentleman's appearance at White's, nor could he fathom why Hasting would give it to him to hold on to unless he wanted him to trade it for the Rockingham, which he expected was the case, considering he was to take the item with him when he went to see Whitmore; however, another point that he could not fathom, was, why, after giving him such an item, he would not have sent along direct commands concerning it.

But as always, Hasting was as vague as a smitten school girl about her age; therefore, Liles assumed, he was to determine his boss's intentions for the package himself, which irritated him excessively. How in the world should he know what the man had in mind? Regardless of Hasting's intended intentions, he read the letter many times prior to the delivery of his sherry and numerous times thereafter. In fact, his brow held such a quizzical scowl that the attendant procured two more snifters without so much as being asked, which was a politeness expected by those who frequented White's. Liles, however, in his current state of mind, thought very little of it.

Later, back at his inn, he informed those good people of his change in plans. "I shall be leaving at first light! Be sure to have my horse and carriage made ready," he commanded still irritated that on the very day of his arrival to London he had to prepare to leave again.

"I was understood to think that you would be staying with us for some length of time," the innkeeper mumbled, feeling ill-used and at a loss concerning the man's quick departure.

"My plans have been drastically changed. Make sure, if you please, that all is made ready! I cannot be detained."

"As you say, sir," the innkeeper responded much confused but truly no more so than Liles was himself.

A straw slipped between his thin lips, a queer eye for detail, and a sizable, crumpled letter that he constantly referred to, Ripling, Hasting's man, held the fourth of Hasting's letters, and, knowing his employer as he did, Ripling flew into action. The carriage must be cleaned and checked, the wheels and straps tightened, the horses, a matched set of chestnut bays, must be brushed, well-fed, and rested in preparation for a summons Hasting told Ripling was sure to come within days of receiving his letter, if, Hasting added, not sooner.

When questioned by the groom about the preparations, Ripling, who rarely spoke, had nothing to say. A shrug of his sinewy shoulders was the only response given to his underlings for his strange behavior. They, however, knew from experience to obey the few words that did proceed out of the man's mouth; therefore, the carriage, spit-polished and gleaming with Ripling handling the ribbons, was ready when the call came to disembark.

Gundy, captain of his own sailing vessel, often received missives from Hasting. In fact, it was Gundy's job to export and import items, be them large or small as Hasting required. On occasion, Hasting required a hull full of casks filled with liquids Gundy didn't ask about, a load of English tea sets, or some such similar items, and when the need arose, Gundy even transported the occasional passenger. Elinore, Hasting's daughter, often times traveled upon Gundy's vessel, and her room upon the craft was finer situated than the captain's.

Gundy, however, surmised from the contents of the letter that her cabin would not be required upon this particular voyage. "After you pick up the load of Spode China from Liverpool, get to the docks at Brighton. Expect a passenger. The gentleman or gentlemen (and I use that term loosely) delivering your passenger will expect a payment for their efforts. Pay twice whatever sum is named. The passenger, who will, no doubt, be a little under the weather when he is escorted to the docks by his 'friends' will be taken along with the load of China to the port at Surat. If he should like transport back to England, which I expect he will, he must prove his meddle AND HIS HUMILITY in a manner that seems genuine to you. As always, my name is not to be mentioned."

With his orders in hand, Gundy began to make ready his ship for travel. As used to such orders as any underling, he was prepared for departure within a reasonable space of time. Taking himself off to Liverpool, he knew Hasting's schemes were time sensitive, therefore, he was sure to be sitting at the dock in Brighton in good time to meet his cargo.

∞ ∞ ∞

The next letter, Hasting's sixth, arrived at an establishment in London. Within a short amount of time, it landed upon a portly fellow's desk. That man read the letter, checked his calendar, and began to make arrangements for his holiday at the Brighton seaside. First his higher-ups were applied to, next he was required to answer numerous questions about his intentions. Finally, after some haggling, it was agreed that he would be given the time he requested. Thankful that such an uncomfortable meeting was at a close, a note was quickly scribbled upon a scrap of paper, sealed, and sent it to be franked.

The return missive itself was brief. Considering the author of it, it was no surprise. However, with the sending of the letter and the promise to perform all the necessary actions required by Hasting, the sender would no longer be in the Hasting's debt. His promise to offer aid would be fulfilled, and he would never be required to perform any other duties in England or abroad for the man, who had, at one time, saved his life from certain peril.

∞ ∞ ∞

Next, Conley, a man of no particular means and even less reputation, manners, and breeding, pulled from a tray of bills a letter addressed to himself in an unknown hand. Upon opening it and seeing that it was from Hasting and about his daughter, that man yelled belligerently to the only servant left him, "Prepare a horse! I ride to Manchester on the marrow!"

"Sir?" his servant, Demps, replied, knowing his employer had neither money, nor a horse, nor would anyone with any knowledge of him allow him credit or a means to transport himself regardless of how much he might desire it.

"And where should I find this...horse?" Demps asked much offended by the idea of another failed attempt to get some foolish chit with a fortune out from under the eyes of her watchful parents.

"BE CREATIVE!" Conley yelled back. "Damn it, man! Make ready our departure! My luck has finally turned—Demps—just as I told you it would!"

"Our departure?" Demps replied with a raised brow and an obvious scoff, "I shall not be accompanying you! I've done with your escapades."

"I can't very well show up at a lady's door without a personal attendant, now can I? Come, Demps! I promise this adventure will not end in ruin!"

"Everything you set your hand to falls to ruins!" was that man's dry reply.

"Not this venture! Look, I have a letter from Hasting about his daughter! He gives me leave to address her!"

"Who might he be?" Demps asked drolly with a flick of his hand through the air, signifying his disinterest.

"Who is Hasting? Are you daft? He's only the richest, socially admired, nabob in all of England and abroad. His family is quite well established, an old name, a great family seat, and land. His father, however, over extended himself when he was young, leaving the family lands in decline and the manse in ill-repair. So what do you suppose this bloke Hasting does?" Conley asked with a flick of his finger upon the letter, agog that he was being applied to and by Hasting, no less.

Not knowing the answer, Demps bobbed his head to the side questioningly, spurning Conley on. "He hires himself out to the *East India Trading Company* and makes it his goal to reestablish his family fortune. The man's made well over 60,000 thousand pounds and, I dare say, will leave it all to his only child, a DAUGH-TER!"

Being unable to school his features into anything respectful, Demps nearly chuckled. "Is the man daft? Why would he give you leave to address her?" he asked in surprised shock, drawing out the word you with great emphasis.

"Perhaps you have forgotten, Demps," Conley began with the same slow smile that made the young ladies swoon, "I come from one of the longest respected names in England, and should I be bereft of one very ill-liked cousin, I will inherit the title of Baron and join the nobility of both England and Ireland!

Seeing, as did all the girls Conley had triumphed over, that he was exceptionally handsome and able to ooze charm when it suited him, Demps softened his reserve, thinking perhaps this Hasting girl was a dowd and easily dazzled by a handsome dandy offering her attention, so he asked, "Have you met this girl?"

"Lawd no, she's been kept away from good society. Probably as round as a pig, but so is her purse, eh?" Conley surmised with a grin as he popped Demps in the ribs. "Girls like her are an easy conquest. They've never in their lives entertained hopes of love match. That is how I woo them, and like the dowdy fools they are, they swoon and believe it!"

Still not convinced, Demps shrugged, "I've seen your attempts before, Conley. They never bear fruit!"

"That's only because the girls' fathers catch wind. This one has invited me! Has invited us!" he exclaimed, holding up the letter as proof. "Think of it Demps! SIXTY-THOUSAND POUNDS! Property. Horses. Descent food again. We'll be swimming in funds," Conley promised as he put his arm around Demps and let him look at the letter.

Ogling over the absurdity of it, Demps could not deny that Hasting had invited him to his Manchester home to visit his daughter.

"And look at this!" Conley continued, showing him the post-mark. "The old man is in Calcutta!" he added, popping the letter with his other hand when another fact proved to be in their favor. "The chit lives in Manchester!"

When Demps failed to notice that as an ingenious stroke of good fortune, Conley added, "Gretna Green is a short jaunt from Manchester! I tell you, Demps, it could not be more perfect!" A smile covered Conley's face, exposing his perfect teeth and brightening his sparking blue eyes, which contrasted against the creamy white of his skin and stark blackness of his hair, sideburns and brows, reminding Demps just how dazzling Conley could be when he elected to be so.

After some little thought, in which Demps examined his other options, he finally conceded. "I expect then we shall need two horses, or do you desire an equipage of some sort?" he asked, making Conley clap his hands with joy and slap him heartily upon his back!

"Horses! We can each of us ride to where we are headed," he answered excitedly. "It is a long journey, but we are young and excellent horsemen."

"As you say," Demps replied, but inwardly he hoped the outcome would be far better than the last escapade they'd been on. That one ended in a foiled attempt to transport an heiress to Gretna Green in a stolen hack.

∞ ∞ ∞

In Manchester, Ichabod's last epistle arrived, causing the greatest perturbation yet and this to his only child, a daughter, Elinore, Ellie to him, whom he had left in a massive manor house in Manchester for the summer while he returned unaccompanied to Calcutta to accomplish some vague task he'd told his daughter only he could perform.

With the letter held tightly in her clinched fist, Ellie stalked purposefully from the confines of her personal salon, and, refusing the more ladylike method of acquiring one's servants, yelled down the central stairwell in tones that could only be described as—livid. "Eldridge, I have need of you!" she screeched.

Recognizing her irate tone and knowing, after having served the girl her entire life, how infrequent such attacks were, Eldridge's interest was instantly piqued, making him stop his conversation with the housekeeper and excuse himself with a regal nod of his head and the words, "If you will excuse me?"

Climbing the central staircase two steps at a time, the faithful retainer entered into the lady's rose salon without his usual knock. "Miss Ellie?" he inquired with a sideways tilt of his head.

"I shall need my trunks brought to my rooms this instant, and the carriage equipped to travel to Kent on the morrow!" she told her butler, looking deceptively striking in a cinnamon colored muslin gown.

As she bent her tall, thin frame forward over the missive she'd received from her father, Ichabod Hasting, her thick auburn hair, which she wore piled upon her head, threatened to tear itself loose from its combs. Already many stray strands had removed themselves from their confines and curled becomingly around her ears, framing her delicate face and brightening her brilliant green eyes, which as she spoke, clouded over with a seething layer of wrath.

Seeing a paper in her grasp and knowing her sire's ability to cause irritation, Eldridge asked, "I expect that is a letter from your father?"

"How astute you are! And yes, of course it is from my father, and, as always, I have no idea what worm has gotten into his brain!" she balked.

"Does he leave any instructions for me, mam?"

"Not a one, and the ones he has left for me, I discredit as the words of a madman."

"I should think you would do well to listen to him, Miss Elinore. You know as well as I his schemes always have a way of turning a profit."

"Yes, he is a great man of business. This scheme; however, I would be required to pay for and that with my own sanity. He might as well have me become an attendant at Bedlam or, perhaps it is his next residency! Who else but a madman would send some cad all of England loathes to our door?"

The elderly man, although perplexed, answered with a nod and these words, "Of course, madam."

"Oh pooh Eldridge! That man could tell you bury me in the garden, and your only response would be, 'Yes, of course, sir!'"

"I am astonished at you, Miss Ellie!" Eldridge began with a mischievous grin upon his well-aged face before adding, "I should think I would ask him how deep!"

Breaking out in a fit of the giggles, Ellie replied, "If I were you, Eldridge, I'd duck!" Doing as he was bid, the man barely missed being pegged by the lady's shoe.

"You see, miss, I've learned a thing or two working in this house," he told her retrieving her footwear.

"Yes, most of which is to be obstinate!" She exclaimed with a smile. "You are a horrid sort of man!" she laughed.

"Yes, Miss Ellie, so you've often told me," he answered before shuffling himself out of the room, a happy smirk lifting the corners of his lips.

If you liked this sample of The Runaway Betrothal please purchase it in either print (Only available at Amazon.com) or in one of its many ebook formats from your favorite retailer.

∞ ∞ ∞

Coming in 2021

The Memory Library: A Gothic Novel

The Romantic Fantasies of a Lonely Girl: A Regency Romance